The Mucklington Murders

D1808210

A PC Bailey Mystery

By

Christopher Mills

The Mucklington Murders

This book is a work of fiction
and except in the cases
where historical fact
or actual place names are used,
any resemblance to actual persons,
living or dead,
is purely coincidental.

Other books in the PC Bailey series

'Murder on Safari'

Who Killed Santa Claus?

Available on Amazon in paperback or Kindle version

www.amazon.co.uk

About this story and the author......

I have been involved in the business of performing Murder Mystery evenings for over twenty-five years with my company Murder by Design. During that time, I have written and produced over forty plots which we have presented in over 800 performances to an estimated 50,000 guests.

As with all PC Bailey mysteries, this book is based on a murder mystery plotline written by me that I give to the team of actors who use it to create their interpretation of the character they are portraying. This is a current, professional plotline and there is every chance that the story you are about to read is being enacted by us as a murder mystery improvisation somewhere in the country for real.

The wording of the clues and the names of the main characters used in this book are identical to those in the murder mystery plotline.

Of course we don't actually kill anyone. That never goes down well with guests, particularly over dinner, and even more so if they have paid for the privilege.

I created and have always played the part of PC Bailey and have great pleasure in handing him over to you to read the backstory of my favourite bumbling copper.

I hope that you enjoy discovering the plot and just 'whodunnit' as much as I have enjoyed writing it and as much as our guests have enjoyed and continue to enjoy seeing the plot revealed over the course of an evening, usually over a wonderful dinner and some fine wine.

Christopher Mills
August 2015

For

Karen, Oliver, Louis and Mollie-Mae

The Mucklington Murders

Chapter One

'Careful! How many times must I tell you?'

'Sorry Mrs, but these stairs is tricky 'specially with all this stuff on 'em.'

The 'Mrs' the reply was aimed at was Lady Buffy Manger, who was currently leaning her exquisitely carved body, over the exquisitely carved handrail at the top of the main staircase, screaming orders to the motley assemblage of staff, rallied from their normal duties, to assist in the transportation of her husband, their employer, Lord Marmaduke Manger, the seventh Earl of Banstead, after he had suddenly taken ill following a nasty encounter with a nail that had been carelessly left sticking out of his chair. The result of said encounter was that he was now being manhandled up his own grand staircase, in a canvas stretcher left over from when the British Army, in the late summer of 1916, had commandeered this fine stately home known as Manger Hall, and used it as a hospital to care for casualties returning from the Somme. Buffy Manger had not been 'in residence', as she liked to put it, at the time of the army occupation. She was after all, a respectable number of years younger than her husband, though the exact number of years varied depending on who she was talking to, and how good her memory was at the time. There were many people in the picturesque village of West Mucklington Parva who, when in the company of their closest friends and well out of the earshot of the 'Lady of the Manor', would comment at how much it grated when she made her 'in residence' remark. For in truth, most of the ladies of the village believed that Buffy was far from the woman she claimed to be, with her purports of a classical education at Cheltenham Ladies' College and a Swiss finishing school to boot. The ladies were very much more of the opinion that the only time anyone in her family had been to Cheltenham was to the racecourse. In short, mutton dressed as lamb, but this mutton had married well and was a living illustration of the - 'golden rule'- those who have the gold, make the rules, and she ruled this house with an iron fist, clad in the finest cashmere gloves.

But Buffy Manger didn't care very much whether the 'ladies' of this little village liked her or not. She had met Lord Manger almost ten years ago when she was sent on an errand by her employer to pick up a painting that he had restored by a small company called Schminkler's who had their workshop near Regent's Park in London. When she arrived there, she knocked and walked in but found no one in the waiting area so walked through to the office and stopped in the doorway when she heard Mr Schminkler talking to another person in the room. Buffy edged closer unsure whether to wait or make her presence known. While she was deliberating, the other man noticed her and stopped his conversation. Instead he stood up straight and admired the view, Buffy Cleminson was a good-looking woman after all. Schminkler, sensing the change in his guest looked up and, on noticing Buffy, he beckoned to her to come in. He quickly introduced her to his good friend Lord Marmaduke Manger. Call it chemistry, call it love at first sight but the two of them seemed to hit it off from the start. They both discovered that they had the same taste for jazz music and he started to make excuses to spend more time in London than at his family estate in the West Country. Buffy was convinced that this was all too good to be true and that he was probably already married to some frumpy upper-class lady but Buffy's heart melted when he assured her that the closest he had ever yet come to marriage was being engaged some ten years or so beforehand but his fiancée had been tragically killed in a boating accident and that he hadn't really looked at another woman. They were married at the church of St Julian's in West Mucklington Parva within six months and she took up her position as the lady of the manor at Manger Hall and had never looked back.

The stretcher party had successfully negotiated the quarter landing but not before clattering the ends of the stretcher poles into the plant stand causing a 1905 Nelson Centenary Jug, with sterling silver rim by Royal Doulton, to wobble alarmingly. Vaughton, Lord Manger's stoical Butler, who was shouldering a pole at the feet end of the operation looked up and, although it was impossible to make out her features from where he stood, because her upper body was silhouetted in spring sunlight streaming in through the leaded roof light over the stairwell, he knew she was giving him one of her best withering looks.

'Vaughton! You may disagree with me about that jug being a collector's piece. In fact, I am aware that only last Thursday, you remarked to the housemaid that if it were to fall during dusting, it would 'not be the greatest loss to the family', but I like it and there it shall stay. Now pick up your end of the stretcher and get 'is Lordship up 'ere double quick, alright?'

Vaughton maintained his composure and only someone who had known him for a very long time would have detected the almost imperceptible flicker at the corner of his eye belying his irritation at her Ladyship's comment. He made a mental note to have a quiet word with the housemaid about conversations that took place below stairs remaining below stairs, and issued a curt instruction under his breath to the other members of staff involved in this logistical nightmare of transporting his Lordship. 'Keep it level at the front; one more flight and we will be up to the first floor where things will undoubtedly be a lot easier. You heard her ladyship; mind the furniture and his Lordship, especially if you value your present employment!'

After another five minutes of manoeuvring, the party reached the first floor, where Buffy barked new commands at them to adjust bearer positions to one man front and back and then continued along the East landing to where Vaughton now stood, having gone on ahead, to open the walnut veneered double doors leading into the ante chamber of Lord Manger's bedroom. Buffy brushed past him with not so much as a look and opened the inner doors revealing the main room.

'Come on in, get him on the bed quickly now. I can't believe it has taken that long to get one bloke up the apple and pears...I mean the staircase, it's just a little joke that me and 'Marmy'...er, his Lordship, like to play. I pretend to be a common girl, it makes him smile.' Just then 'Marmy' raised his arm and feebly gestured towards the bed. The party took the hint and advanced.

Hogarth, the front stretcher bearer, just twenty years old, dressed in the distinctive green and black livery of an under footman, looked wide-eyed as he entered the room. Until fifteen minutes ago he had been gainfully employed assisting with the arrangements for the grand village meeting taking place this evening. He had, in fact, just completed carrying through the last of the larger vases which had been strategically placed, under strict direction of Mrs Manger, to create 'red flowers in every direction' or 'flowers here, flowers there, flowers every bloomin' where!' as Gertrude, the scullery maid, had remarked, as she shoved the last of the scarlet blooms into the vase. Hogarth thought back to the first time he had seen her, that winter's day last December, when he had heard muffled knocking on the scullery door and opened it to find a young woman wrapped up tightly against the biting cold, her gloved hand still raised mid-knock, asking where she might find Mrs Glenworth the Housekeeper.

As he set the vase down, he found himself smiling at Gertrude's comment. He liked her and he had an idea that she had taken a shine to him as well because, on more than one occasion, he had caught her stealing a sideways glance as they had passed each other going about their daily routines. He had only arrived at Manger Hall himself on the hottest day of last summer.

Vincent Hogarth had been born in 1918 as the Allies made their last great push for victory his mother made hers, to produce her only child and promptly died from the effort. His father John Hogarth blamed his new son for taking away the love of his life and so, within hours of entering the world, he was all alone except for John's older brother named Roy, a ne'er-do-well who no one had heard of in over ten years, and an aged aunt named Olive Birch who took him home to Birmingham to live with her.

In her working life, Olive had been a secretary for a manufacturing company; John Mitchell, whose dominance as the world leader in producing writing pens was evident from the sign which read 'John Mitchell Pens' fixed above the entrance of an impressive red-brick factory in Newhall Street in the City Centre. She was a well-read woman who had been careful with her money and rented well-appointed rooms in Colmore Row, a conveniently short walk from her place of work and where she would push up her sash windows in the lounge and sit on a summer's evening and listen to the choir practising in Birmingham Cathedral across the street. She was passionate about the arts and had always thought that if a boy was born into the Hogarth family, that he should take the name of her favourite artist, Vincent van Gogh, in the hope that with the name of Vincent Hogarth, he would have a good prospect of following the arts himself. Of course, she realised that in truth, just because you name a child after a couple of talented artists, it doesn't follow that he will be able to paint, but she believed that people often treated people differently because of the way they dressed, spoke and their name and so she hoped this would at least give him a head start in that direction.

Vincent had happy memories of being met from school by his kindly Aunt and taken off to an art gallery or a museum or sometimes they would walk down the flight of steps opposite the Mitchell factory to the Birmingham and Fazeley Canal which ran under Newhall Street, and they would sit on the canal bank and watch the narrow boats negotiate the two locks situated each side of the bridge. His Aunt would produce paper and pencils and encourage him to draw what he saw. It was while he was sat quietly drawing by the canal that Olive had broken the news to him that his father had died of lung cancer. Vincent was working on a particularly difficult view of the river arches at the time and had taken on board the information and stored it away without so much as a break in the sweeping line on the paper.

Olive was delighted to discover that her encouragement was working because it was clear to everyone that this boy had a talent to draw and, long before he had begun to grow into a young man, she had begun to make plans to send him to work as a junior in an art studio. Vincent's future was taking shape when, like a bolt out of the blue, everything changed after a couple of mischievous young lads set off some Chinese firecrackers they had found left over from bonfire night under a horse and cart, startling the poor animal and causing it to bolt. The driver of the horse was able to grab hold of the side of the cart, and even managed to climb back into the driving seat, but the stricken animal was unstoppable and careered on down the road, just making the left turn off Lionel Street where the cart mounted the kerb and ploughed into the front of Smith's the Greengrocer's display, sending fruit and vegetables bouncing along the pavement and rolling into the road. In the pandemonium that followed, with the cart overturning and the driver, who had a lucky escape, trying to calm down the horse now trapped between the broken shafts, no one noticed the smart brown handbag that lay beneath the wheels on the pavement, and it wasn't until after many willing volunteers in a coordinated shove had managed to right the cart, that they found the broken body of Olive Birch.

Vincent's life changed there and then. Everyone was very sympathetic of course, but what he didn't realise was that Roy had reappeared on the scene five years earlier and had conned his sister, who always worried about who would care for Vincent if anything happened to her, into making a Will that passed over all her worldly goods to Roy, on the condition that he looked after the boy if she died before he became an adult. The horse and cart incident was unquestionably unlucky for Olive and unexpectedly fortuitous for Roy who stepped out of the shadows, happily taking the money and begrudgingly taking the boy off to the West Country where, over the course of the next five years, he conveniently forgot his agreement to look after Vincent and left him to fend for himself for most of the time, while he took up residence in the local public houses until almost all the money had gone. Things were looking very bad for Vincent when Fate took a hand and Roy, in a drunken stupor on a particularly blustery night, took a wrong turning on the way back to the hovel he had found for him and his charge, and stumbled over the edge of the road on Gannet Head and freefalled the next two hundred and fifty-three feet on to an outcrop of particularly solid rocks which arrested his fall at the bottom of the sheer cliffs.

For the second time in his lifetime, Vincent found himself alone, but he had been industrious while left on his own all day, doing odd jobs around the village. He listened intently to the policeman who knocked on his door and told him what had happened to Roy without a single emotion crossing his face. When the officer enquired what he was going to do now, he informed him that he already had employment, working locally, and that he would be alright, and indeed he was. He had built himself a good reputation of being an honest, hardworking young man able to turn his hand to just about anything, and by the spring of 1937 he had come to the attention of the staff at Manger Hall and, in the sweltering summer of that same year, he found himself being offered a permanent job as part of Lord Manger's retinue as an under footman. His thoughts came back to the present and how he should make a plan to ask Gertrude, indirectly of course, if she might consider coming along with him and some of the other staff, on their day off, to the Regal to watch the latest film and then fish and chips from the 'Jolly Fat Fryer' in the high street....too late, he had daydreamed too long and Mrs Manger enquired in his direction, 'and what do you find so amusing, Horath!?'

'It's Hogarth ma'am, and I was just thinking how good these flowers look' replied the young man, impressed at himself with his snappy response.

'Really?' Buffy had not expected the reply, and found herself on the back foot. 'Yes, well they should do. I arranged the whole thing.'

Hogarth nodded and thought about saying that he was pretty sure it was the sweet little maid that had arranged the flowers but thought better of it. Mrs Manger didn't bother to acknowledge his nod in any case. 'And the reason for the red flowers is because of the painting that Lord Manger bought for me at the auction last week.'

The under footman tried to look as if he understood though in truth he didn't. Buffy continued.

'The painting is by Mr Salvador Dali. It's called "Female Figure with Head of Flowers". His Lordship said it reminded him of me, what with my beautiful auburn hair, though I think it's more likely because of my figure.' She made a noise in her screechy tones that sounded more like nails on a blackboard than laughter. Then, snapping her gaze back to him, she continued with his education in art as if she was an expert on the subject. 'You do know then, that if your name is Hogarth, that you have the same name as a famous artist I presume?'

The young man picked his words carefully because he knew only too well how easy it was to offend her Ladyship if she thought you were being cleverer than she was, which he thought wasn't very difficult to do. He thought back a few weeks of Mr Johnson the handyman, who made the mistake of suggesting it might be a clever idea to wait for the wind to die down before chopping down a silver birch tree that Buffy had decided she didn't want around her ornamental pond any longer. She insisted he got on with the work without delay and when the tree fell on her new pergola poor Johnson got his marching orders there and then. 'No ma'am,' he replied. 'Thank you for letting me know.'

Lady Manger looked set to make another comment when she was interrupted by an uproarious bellow emanating from the direction of the Ballroom. Hogarth followed her as she hurried along the corridor where the sounds of other voices calling for help were joining in. As they entered through the large double doors, they found Lord Manger writhing around on the parquet floor clutching his rear flanks.

Now less than twenty minutes later, after Mrs Manger had shouted for 'someone to fetch the Doctor', and Mr Vaughton had taken charge of organising a stretcher, and Lady Manger made the decision to move her stricken husband up to his bedroom, here he was, Hogarth, a lowly under footman, carrying his Lordship on a stretcher into his private quarters, an area of Manger Hall that he had never even in his wildest expectations thought he would ever see.

The stretcher was placed on the bed and, with some effort, Marmaduke was rolled off and under the blankets. He was visibly sweating and his face was turning purple. He had been bellowing when he had first sat on the nail but as time passed, the bellows had subsided to groans, which had given way to just occasional noises of discomfort. Buffy made much out of plumping his pillows and then, after reassuring everyone that his Lordship was just suffering from shock and would be up and about in no time, she shooed them all from the room, except for the chamber maid, a rather short ugly girl named Maude, who had arrived with a jug of water, as instructed by the Butler. The maid nodded that she understood Buffy's strict instructions to look in on his Lordship every hour without fail, and with a rather untidy curtsey, and after one last concerned look his Lordship, she hurriedly left the room.

Buffy surveyed her own handywork with a look of approval, 'There, all done, I'm sure that should make you feel a good deal more comfortable my dear. Now, of course, I will have to make the welcoming speech and outline my - I mean, *our*- proposal for Rose's money. I am your wife and the Lady of the House after all, so I'm sure I'll cope. You just rest and leave everything to me.' She pecked her own hand and then leaned over him and placed it on his cheek, which was both red and waxy, but she didn't seem to notice his condition at all. 'Goodnight sweet prince.' She turned around at the doorway and looked over her shoulder at the prone figure in the bed. She had pulled the dark green heavy brocade coverlet up to her husband's neckline, just leaving his head nestling in the pillows which, as they radiated out in all directions, made him look a little like a giant daisy. She smiled and left the room.

When Marmaduke Manger was left alone in his bedroom by his apparently loving wife, he was already barely conscious and, long before the Doctor had surfaced from the pub and made his way to the Manor House, and just before the ugly maid had returned to make her very first visit to his bedside, and before a member of His Majesty's Constabulary would stand and look into his face, the Seventh Earl of Banstead would be dead.

*

Police Constable John Bailey watched Buffy Manger descend the stairs and then stepped forward to enquire about the wellbeing of her husband.

'Oh, he's quite alright. I think it's a mixture of shock and embarrassment if you ask me. Anyway, I have sent for

Doctor Macdonald, just to give him the once over, though at this time of the day it could be a while before he'll surface from the Pig & Whistle, so don't hold your breath, constable.'

'Well that is good news. Er, not that the Doctor might take a while to get here you understand, but that your husband is going to be fine.'

'Quite. Now, unless there is anything else, I really must get on. The servants take so long to do anything at the best of times and when you must retain certain staff, at the insistence of one's husband, that are as completely useless as Kate, then you need to keep on top of things otherwise nothing gets done. We do have a rather important meeting tonight which I am sure you are aware of and everything must be right!' With that, Buffy made off in the direction of the entrance hall, shouting and pointing at members of staff as she moved, the sound of exasperation ringing out in her shrill voice.

PC Bailey was, indeed, aware of the meeting this evening. That was the reason why he was here in the first place. He had arrived at the Police Station in Exeter at half past eight this morning, and hadn't even made it half way through his mug of tea before his desk sergeant called out from along the corridor, 'Bailey, a word please.'

He put down his mug, because the Chief Inspector was very particular about the image that his constables gave to the public as they walked around the station; he liked them to look professional and thought that swanking around with a mug of tea gave the impression that they were lax. Bailey had learned this lesson the hard way and had never forgotten it. He straightened his uniform and walked briskly to the front desk.

'Bailey, yes. A little job, nothing too taxing, right up your street, really.'

'Oh right, Sarge, that'll be handy getting off home at the end of my shift, then.'

'What will?' the sergeant peered at the constable with a quizzical look.

'The job you're giving me, it'll be handy.'

'I'm not really following you, Bailey, and as I haven't told you what I want you to do yet I can't see - oh Lord.' The desk sergeant stopped his conversation mid-sentence and clapped his hand to his head as he took a breath. 'The penny has just dropped with me. No, Bailey, when I said that it was up your street, I meant that as a figure of speech.'

'Right, Sarge.'

'What I meant was, it's a job that will suit you. I didn't mean that it was actually in your - oh never mind, let's just give you the details and get you on your way, eh?'

'Right, Sarge,' Bailey replied for the second time, though it didn't look as if he had grasped any of the last conversation. His sergeant shook his head slowly and then, leaning closer to Bailey across the desk, he began.

'There is a village meeting later this evening up at West Mucklington Parva....,' Bailey began to raise his hand but the sergeant continued 'and before you say it, I know you probably don't know where that is at the moment, but don't worry, I have a car that will take you there. '

Bailey lowered his hand again back to the desk 'Right, Sarge. A village meeting you say?'

'Yes, Bailey. Apparently, a widow from the village passed away about a month ago and when they read her Will, it turns out the old girl left a fair bit of money, over a hundred thousand pounds, in fact, and she wants the villagers to decide what to do with it. The meeting is taking place this evening and there's going to be people from the village giving speeches on their ideas of what to do with the money. Then, at the end of the evening, everyone has a vote and the idea that gets the most votes gets the money.'

'Oh, so I'll be working this evening as well, then, Sarge?'

'No, you won't. I just want you up there this afternoon; Lord Marmaduke Manger is a friend of the Chief Inspector and he is worried that some of the villagers might get a bit rowdy because not everyone is happy with some of the ideas, so the Chief has agreed to send along a policeman to attend, just for show more than anything else. They are having a rehearsal, a run through of the proceedings, if you like, at two o-clock and I want you to see how it goes, make some notes, and then pass the information on to Constable Fogg when he relieves you at five o'clock. Is that all clear?'

'Yes, Sarge – all clear on that.'

'Good. The car will be here in half an hour to collect you so finish up your tea and I haven't seen those notes yet on Mrs Manchip's lad and those tractor parts that he had in his shed belonging to Specklingcote Farm, I'd like to have them before you go...-if you've done 'em of course?'

'Oh, yes, Sarge, I have them in the duty room. As you always say, I'm not good at everything but there's one thing I am good at.' Bailey turned and walked off down the corridor, his blurred reflection dancing along the brown and cream gloss painted walls, passing the bottom of the stone stairs leading to the Chief Inspector's office and disappeared through a doorway to the right into the duty room, leaving a clear view to the far end of the corridor where another set of stairs led down to the cells. The desk sergeant watched Bailey disappear and thought to himself, 'yes, Bailey. As I always say there is one thing you're good at...I just can't remember for the life of me what it is.'

Chapter Two

'Well, you're going to be for it now, Harry. What were you thinking of?'

'What for, Katie? I haven't dun nuthin.'

'You left them nails sticking out of the chair and now his Lordship's gone and sat on one of 'em and taken to his bed with the shock. When the missus Manger gets hold, I wouldn't want to be in your shoes!'

Harry Clott thrust his hands deep into the pockets of his well-worn moleskin trousers. His old leather belt dipped across his belly. It held firm, but forced his pelvis and his shoulders forward, making him look like the gaunt and bent figure of a much older man. His head hung down facing his tattered and scuffed leather boots that had seen the first polish applied to them this morning in a good few years. Despite the appearance his present mood was creating, Harry was in fact a young man of twenty-four, or at least that was the age that he had been told he was. He wasn't entirely sure himself because working out how old a person was involved counting, and that wasn't something he was particularly good at. Well, not if it involved numbers that he couldn't do on his fingers.

He was standing against the wall of one of the sheds that stood along the west wall of the walled garden at Manger Hall. This was Harry's favourite place, well, apart from the river bank where he often sat when the weather was nice, with Katie, his friend. She was a maid here at the house and that's who he was deep in conversation with now. Katie, as he called her, though her real name was Kate, had told him that she was the same age as him. He liked that because it meant that she was neither older nor younger. It also meant if he needed to know how old he was, he just needed to ask Katie how old she was and then he knew, though sometimes she used to tease him and tell him that a young man should never ask a lady how old she was, which he thought was a strange thing, because his father, who was the head gardener here at the Hall, had always taught him that if you didn't know the answer to something then the best thing to do was to ask someone who did.

Apart from her teasing, Katie was a good friend and sometimes, when they both had the same half day off, they would catch the bus and go into Exeter and watch a film at the picture houses in Sidwell Street, where there was a choice of the ABC or the Odeon. Harry liked them both but the Odeon was the newest one and a bit posher and the Manager would stand in his immaculate dinner suit in the foyer and stare in horror at Harry's 'bestest' clothes and suggest that he sat on a newspaper because 'it would be more comfortable for him'. They had watched 'Top Hat' just last week; Katie had sat through the whole film holding his arm and, staring at the screen as the man and the woman danced together, she had told him their names but all he could remember now was that the man was called Fred.

'But I din't mean to leave them nails sticking out, it's just that they was longer than the bit of wood I knocked 'em in to.'

Kate put her hand softly on his shoulder, she knew he hadn't meant to hurt anyone, how could he? He didn't have a nasty bone in his whole body; it was an accident pure and simple. 'I know that, Harry, but you should have used some shorter nails, and then it would have been alright. Anyway, what have you done with the chair now?'

'Mr Vaughton looked at all the chairs after what 'appened, and he took some of 'em away and got one of the men to bring some that I 'adn't been mending.'

'Well that's good 'Arry, at least no one else will get 'urt. You try an' find out where them chairs have gone and you can mend them properly, and then maybe people won't be so cross. I'll help you if you like?'

'Thanks Katie, you know I want you to help.'

Kate Rimehill was tall for a girl, and with her raven hair pinned tightly under a mop cap, her good bones and fair complexion made a striking combination that was not unpleasant to the eye by a long chalk. She had become friends with Harry soon after arriving at Manger Hall almost five years ago when she had just turned fifteen, taking up the position of Housemaid which had been arranged for her through her Headmistress, a rather eccentric woman in her nineties who ruled with an iron will, and who had informed Kate when she was old enough to understand, all that she knew about her parents, which as it turned out was very little. Kate had remained at the school until she came here to Manger Hall. Perhaps it was the fact that both Harry and Kate had positions amongst the lower staff, or perhaps it was that, even with her private schooling, she wasn't what anyone would consider an academic. But it was more likely that the reason why they had become such good friends was because Kate seemed to look beyond Harry's slowness and he seemed oblivious to her quirky, clumsy nature and that suited the both of them.

Chapter Three

'Clott!' Marmaduke Manger's voice caused the head gardener's dim-witted son to attempt to stand smartly to attention instead of his naturally awkward posture. The result was somewhere in between but it was the best Clott could muster at such short notice. 'What on earth has happened to my riding boots?' The Lord of the Manor stomped into the scullery with an expression that suggested he might just kill the next living thing he set eyes on. He was clearly dressed ready to go riding in his mustard waistcoat and Harris Tweed riding jacket; the image, however, was incomplete because instead of his off-white jodhpurs disappearing into the top of highly polished riding boots, he was instead holding some rather misshapen boots in his right hand in front of him and a riding crop in the other. He had what could be termed a ruddy complexion at the best of times, but the fact that as he advanced towards him he resembled an Azalea in full bloom. Clott knew the next few minutes were going to be uncomfortable. It would not be unkind to say that Harry Clott wasn't the fastest thinker in the neighbourhood, but even he could read the expression on his Lordship's face to be sure that, if there was a murder about to be committed, he was the most likely candidate to be the victim. Harry recalled there had been an incident which involved the lawn roller and the boots, now being shaken vigorously an inch away from his nose.

'Well, Clott. Speak and the explanation had better be a good one or I swear I'll take this riding crop to your hide,' he said, flicking the short leather crop and making that unmistakable 'whoom' noise that comes when you move thin objects quickly through the air. The noise took Harry back to a time when he and Jim Tucker were having a sword fight with birch twigs that Harry's father had set aside for making repairs to the fence in the water meadow. He remembered that same sound so distinctly and the sharp pain that made him yelp when he got hit across the back of his hand as he failed to parry Jim's arcing shot.

'Ow that flippin' urt!' Harry stopped fighting and sucked at the top of his hand but Jim just laughed even more and swung again, this time catching Harry just above his knee. Thwack!

'Right, that's it Tucker, I'm going to get you for that!'

'Well you have to catch me first 'Arry!' And with that, he took off across the farmyard and out through the bottom gate leading into the field that rolled away from the farm and away down to the river. Well they called it a river because that's what it was but to both boys it was more like a brook or at most a stream because for most of the length of the bottom field you could jump across from one bank to other without much problem at all, even on the bits when it did make an effort to try and be a stream, both boys could still jump it if you took a good run up.

'Well, I'm waiting!'

Clott broke off from his thoughts and tried to focus on Mr Manger who continued to dangle the boots in front of him.

'You see sir, there was this lump of wood.'

'What did you say, Clott? Did you say wood?'

'Yessir, wood sir.'

'What about it?' The crop flicked in his hand .

'Well I was working on building the tables for the big 'do' this evening and I could see that one of the long tables that you pulls the legs out of.'

'Trestles.'

'No, sir, tables'

Marmaduke Manger glowered at the half-wit standing in front and, for the first time ever, he took in his attire. The young man, probably no more than twenty years old, he estimated, not that he really cared, was wearing leather boots that looked as if they had been old in the First World War and surely couldn't be the right size for this slip of a man. His trousers were made of black cloth that had lengths of baling twine tied around them just below the knees. 'What are those for?

'Well you put things on 'em and Mr Vaughton said that he was going to put...'

'No, not the tables, Clott! What are those for, those strings around your legs, what are they for?'

Clott shot a quizzical look at his master. He had not really got the thread of this conversation at all. One minute he was getting ready to take a tongue lashing for what had happened to the riding boots and then his Lordship had started on about trestles or something, and now he wanted to know about the string.

'It's for the mouses sir.'

'Pardon?'

'It's for the mouses sir, it stops them from going up yer trousers when you're in the barn. They can move like summer lightning when they gets cornered and they'll run any way they can and right over yer boots before yer know it, an' if you ain't got no string around your legs, well you are just as likely to have some uninvited guests rummaging where you don't want things with sharp claws and teeth to be rummaging, if yer understands my meaning.'

Marmaduke had lived all his life in this part of the world and although his family and his friends had received a good education and spoke perfect English, he was nevertheless fully able to understand the local dialect of the working classes. 'Ah, yes, I see, well that's very enterprising and functional, though I thought we had cats to keep down the mice?'

'Oh we 'ave sir and a good job they do an' all but there's a lot more mouses than there is cats and so you needs yer own protection.' Clott thought for a moment and then added. 'I suppose yer could have a cat down yer trousers but that could be tricky to walk around with and there would be all hell to pay if a mouse came up yer leg. It don't bear thinking about really!'

'Clott! Enough of this drivel. You mentioned wood, what has wood got to do with my riding boots looking like this?'

'As I was sayin' sir. I needed a good-sized piece of wood to mend the table and I saw the piece on the ground but I couldn't pick it up because the tractor was leaning up against it. But the mud was soft so I gave it a wiggle and I could see that if I wiggled it a lot more it might come free. Anyway, I got ter wigglin' and I got it free and it was just what I was lookin' for so I went back into the shed to nail it to the table and, and that's when I heard the sound...'

'And what sound would that be Clott? Come on, out with it boy.'

'It's 'ard to explain really, like a scrapin' and then a thump.' So, I stopped me nailin' and went back outside and at first I couldn't see anything wrong. But then after I had a think about it, I could see that everythin' wasn't the same as when I went in the shed.'

'Why, what had changed? Is this going to take very much longer Clott?'

'No, sir, I'm nearly there really. Well what had changed was that the tractor wasn't where it had been. Instead it was now down the other end of the yard sittin' half inside tack room.'

'Had someone moved it then Clott? Who was driving it? The tack room you say? Why wasn't I informed about this, where is the stable lad!?'

'No, there wasn't a driver. Tom, who should have bin drivin', came runnin' over to me and said that there was a problem with the braking on the tractor and, well, how was I supposed to know sir?'

'Know what, Clott? For heaven's sake just spit it out!'

'The wood, sir, Tom had put it behind the wheel to stop it from rollin' down the hill but how was I supposed to know? So, when I took it away, well, as I said.'

'And I am to assume that my boots were in the tack room?'

'No sir, luckily they were outside the tack room. I was going to give 'em a good polish, sir, just like you asked. Unluckily, the wheel went right over 'em, sir.'

'Clott, if it wasn't for the sterling service that your father has given to this family over many years, I would take this crop to you first and the see you off this estate.'

'Yessir, thank you, sir.'

'Don't thank me, you fool. Thank your father. But let me tell you, this is your last chance and you will pay half of your wages each week until you have paid for a new pair of boots. Have you got that in your thick head Clott!?'

Lord Manger dropped the squashed boots at Clott's feet and turned and marched back out of the room, slamming the door behind him. He could still be heard muttering under his breath as he made his way back through his house and Harry waited until he was quite sure that he was gone before he picked up the boots and made his way out of the back door leading into the yard. He had decided he would go around to the potting sheds first to check on his seedlings and then best he got on with mending the rest of the tables before he got started on the chairs. When he had counted the chairs that needed mending, -no mean task for Harry-, he knew he might not be able to do his best job if he was going to get it all ready for the practice this afternoon but he thought as long as he tried his best, then everything would be alright. But he would make a special effort to fix Lord Manger's chair, once and for all...

Chapter Four

Reverend Cecil Smeeton winced as he adjusted his sitting position, and thought it was no wonder at all that his congregation had dwindled so much over the last thirty years he had been incumbent here at the parish church of St Julian's in West Mucklington Parva, if the pews in the Lady Chapel were anything to go by. They were, at best, uncomfortable and how anyone sat here for more than an hour was nothing short of remarkable. Yet, as he lifted one side of his buttocks off the hard wooden surface and massaged some life back into them through his robes, he thought about how Rose Stimper had sat in this very pew, year in, year out, and listened to his sermons on every topic from the troubles in Europe to the starving children on the streets of our big cities, his Christmas message and not forgetting the importance of Easter, without so much as a change of expression passing over her gently uplifted, smiling visage. He marvelled at the old woman's tenacity. The more he thought about it, he couldn't ever remember a service when she had not been in attendance, apart from the last month of her life. In fact, it was that he had noticed the empty space where she should have been sitting, that had prompted him at the end of morning service to make the short walk from the church along the cobbled path that wound its way along the edge of the south meadow of Manger Hall and eventually down to the river along the way, passing the picturesque thatched home of Rose Stimper. Of course, this wasn't the first time that he had made the journey, over the years; they had become good friends and he was often a visitor to her home. He remembered that visit, in particular, and how, above the quaint wooden front door hung a hand painted sign which read 'Rose Cottage', and how each side of the door and all the way along the uneven whitewashed walls were rose bushes which at this time of the year were just beginning to show their early buds and promised yet again to cover the front of the building in glorious blooms, as summer approached. He had knocked gently on the black iron knocker fashioned in the shape of a woodpecker and, as he had done so many times before, opened the door and let himself in. Rose never locked her door; she was a firm believer that there wasn't anyone in the world who would do her any harm. Inside, as with most quaint little cottages, the room was dark, even though there were no curtains at the tiny windows. Everything looked neat and in its proper place but there was no sign of the old woman. 'Rose, are you here?' There was no response so he tried again, a little louder this time. 'Rose, are you home? It's me Cecil.' The vicar stood still, straining to hear a response, which came in the form of a click of the latch on the bedroom door which opened, and in shuffled, very slowly, a small bent figure dressed in a dark robe. The face in the robe looked towards the vicar and, even in the gloom, he saw the unmistakable face of Rose Stimper.

'Good morning, Cecil. I was wondering if you would notice that I wasn't there and would come calling.' Rose dragged out a chair from the table and sat down with a heavy exhalation of breath as if the effort of walking was more of a problem than usual.

'Of course, I noticed you weren't there, Rose. This morning's attendance was, shall we say, very scant indeed. Your attendance would have increased the numbers by a quarter.'

'Oh, I see. Well, sit down, Cecil. I have something to tell you, but I will make us some tea first.' She tapped the back of the chair next to hers as she got up from the table and made her way through another door. In a few moments, Cecil could hear water being drawn from the handpump and then the heavy kettle being placed on the range. The small woman reappeared and went to the dresser on the far side of the room, deftly selecting cups, saucers and side plates, before bringing them over and setting them down in front of the vicar as he took his place at the table. 'I'm sure after your efforts this morning, despite the number in the congregation, that you are ready for some refreshment and I have some lovely scones, that I made only yesterday, which will go down quite nicely with a pot of tea.' She shuffled off again, back through the door where the sound of the rapidly heating water was now filling the otherwise silent kitchen. Cecil sat quietly surveying the room. He had sat here many times and looked around the whitewashed walls and the assortment of bunches of dried flowers and cornstalks that had been fixed to the blackened ceiling beams above. At this time of the year, the light hardly managed to creep into the furthest recess of the room, but he could make out the familiar shape of the fire irons to the side of the hearth and the treadle sewing machine that sat in front of the largest window. The sight of the sewing machine reminded him to speak to his curate about the possibility of organising the ladies of the village to make some cushions for the pews. He took the poker from the stand and poked at the hearth, the dull red embers of the fire banked up by the old woman the night before glowed angrily at being disturbed; a few sparks spiralled upwards like miniature fireworks. A short blue flame licked over the coals and the vicar smiled to himself that he had succeeded in rekindling the fire and had brought some much-needed warmth to the room.

'Here is your tea, Cecil, come and sit.'

He felt the gratifying weight of the heavy poker in his hand for a second longer before replacing it on the stand and then joined his host at the table. Rose poured the tea, adding milk and sugar without the need to ask, as she knew his preference only too well, and edged the cup in his direction while indicating to the plate of scones with her free hand.

'So, my dear Rose, what is it that you want to tell me and what caused you to miss this morning's prayers?'

She sipped at her tea, her eyes almost lost in the steam rising from the cup. Then suddenly she replaced it firmly in the saucer, the noise sharp and clear in the silence, as if she had reached a decision, she cleared her throat and fixed her gaze on him. 'The answer is the same for both of your questions Cecil, so I think it is easier if I just get on with it. The fact is I am dying.'

'But that can't be true Rose; you look as well as...' Rose placed her hand on his and held a finger to her lips. Cecil, with shock and bewilderment written across his pale features, protested for a moment longer and then let his old friend continue to speak.'

'It is true. I had it confirmed yesterday at the cottage hospital when I went there for my appointment. Mr Wilkinson is my Consultant, a brilliant young man; he told me that the X-Ray picture clearly shows that I have a very large tumour on my brain. It is very advanced and accounts for the terrible headaches that I have been having these past few months. It is inoperable. There is nothing to be done, Cecil.'

Cecil Smeeton placed his hands on the paper in front of him on which he had been writing his sermon in the Lady Chapel and reflected how, so soon after that fateful meeting with Rose, she had begun to show signs of her illness, and how her absence from services became more frequent and how in just a matter of weeks he had seen Kate, the maid, running towards him in her uniform across the graveyard while he tended some flowers that had fallen over in the heavy rain that had fallen incessantly over the last week. 'Reverend Smeeton! It's Miss Stimper, Rose; she wants you to come over as quickly as you can!' This was the message that she blurted out, bent double, catching her breath from running hard along the cobbled path.

He remembered how he brushed the dirt from his hands and set off, with Kate in tow back, to Rose Cottage, where he went straight in and found Rose lying so still in her bed. He thought he was too late, but her eyes flickered and opened and a weak smile came across her face just as Kate blustered into the room. Cecil ushered her out with a flick of his hand telling her to make herself busy and him a cup of tea and to close the door after her, which she dutifully did. He took Rose's hand; it was warm but looked so limp and small in his upturned palm; traces of the soil still on his hands from his earlier work. He thought how frail she had become and he knew that her time was now and yet, when she spoke, her voice was still strong. He listened to what she wanted to tell him and then she fell quiet and a brief time later, with nothing more than a sigh, she passed across and he knew that he was alone in that tiny bedroom. He gently placed her hand across her chest and called for Kate to send for Doctor Macdonald.

Most of the village turned out for the funeral, many of whom didn't really know Rose at all but wanted to come and pay their respects out of curiosity to the woman who they always knew as 'The Widow' though, as far as anyone knew, she had never been wed. If people had been only curious at Rose's funeral, they certainly became overtly interested in her once her Last Will and Testament was read out by her solicitor James Fitchett of Marlowe, Fitchett and Tump Esquire, in tones that sounded like the end of the world was upon the assembled throng. Rose had stated that her Will should be read from the pulpit of St Julian's on the first convenient Sunday following her funeral and that all the villagers should be invited to attend. She had added a footnote, not to be read out, stating, 'at least dear Cecil will have a good attendance at his service for once'. And so it was that Mr Fitchett read from the Will; *"I Rose Stimper, have made provision for the sum of One Hundred Thousand Guineas to be set aside for the good people born within the village of West Mucklington Parva to put forward their proposals as to what the money should be spent on, for the greater good of the village, and that a grand meeting should be arranged, and the proposals heard, from those who would make such proposals, and each villager should cast their vote, once only, for the proposal that they favour, and that the proposal with the greatest number of votes, should receive the aforementioned money. If there should be any remainder, then the next most popular proposal should receive said remainder and so on until the money has all been allocated."*

The church remained silent for no more than a second and then a cheer went up, followed by enthusiastic clapping; sounds that had not been heard in St Julian's in living memory. Then the murmurings started and continued out of the Nave and into the village square, the bakers, the milk parlour, the farmyards and the public houses. No-one talked of anything else; everyone had an opinion and, with so much money at stake, sadly, but inevitably, people began losing their temper with other villagers whom they hardly knew, their workmates and even their close friends. It would appear, the saying 'The love of money is the root of all evil' was true.

Cecil had stood up in his pulpit on more than one Sunday following the reading, to a greatly reduced congregation, and told people that this money was intended for the benefit of everyone, but some of his words had fallen on deaf ears and there had been many occasions over the weeks leading up to the General Meeting where the outcome of a heated debate was a black eye or a bruise or two. He was glad when, at last, the day of the meeting had finally dawned and it would be settled for good. He had his own proposal, of course, and was quietly confident that he would attract a good proportion of the votes for his ideas. In fact, he was so confident that he was going to refer to thanking his congregation for getting behind his ideas in his next sermon, following the meeting, which he was putting the finishing touches to now and the reason why he was enduring this discomfort. He had welcomed the extra time caused by the rehearsal breaking up early to really polish up his words for both his proposal and his sermon. He looked out of the plain leaded window in the Lady Chapel and saw that the skies were darkening and decided he had better make tracks soon if he was to avoid getting caught in the rain on his way back to Manger Hall. He gathered his things together and made a hurried scribbled note in the side margin of his sermon notes to add in the idea that some of the money could be spent on changing that plain window into a wonderful rose, in stained glass, to commemorate Rose's generosity to the Church where she chose to worship. To be fair to the widow, this was her local church and it was a good nine and a half miles to the next one, but that wasn't the point.

Thinking back to the rehearsal for a moment, he thought of how stupid Harry had been to have left a nail in the chair sticking out and how Marmaduke Manger had been taken ill with the shock of what must have been a very painful experience. It must have been awful and he had watched how the Lord of the Manor had literally leapt into the air with an almighty yell. It was shocking to see and yet he couldn't help smiling that if it should have to happen to anyone, then he was the one who should have received it. He admonished himself for thinking such un-Christian thoughts. He hoped that this fortunate turn of events would make his proposal even more likely to receive the money; another un-Christian thought. He shrugged and made a note to sit on these pews more often as a penance.

Chapter Five

Bailey stepped out from the Police Car at a little after one o'clock, almost an hour before the rehearsal got under way. He leaned in through the door and reminded the driver that he needed to be picked up again at five o'clock. The journey had been unremarkable and he had spent the hour looking out at the grand buildings of Exeter as they gave way to the rolling hills and high Tors of Dartmoor and the huge expanses of bracken that were characteristic of this sometimes wild and unpredictable, yet beautiful, countryside. As they neared their destination, Bailey got his first sight of just how swollen the river had become and, as he passed over the ancient stone bridge that was the only vehicle access on to the Manger Estate, he noted that only the very tops of the arches of the bridge remained visible as the water rushed and gurgled on its way to the open sea.

Manger Hall itself was a fine example of Georgian Architecture with impressive columns supporting the large stone portico over the main entrance. Bailey could see in through the windows into the room beyond and noted the huge chandelier. The front door was open and servants and tradespeople were coming and going at a regular rate, all in preparation for the big meeting later, he guessed. The land on which the Hall was built, had for centuries, been as much a part of the Devon mainland as Exeter itself, but the great river Exe had eventually eroded away the softer ground and where the river once meandered it now swirled around an island. But the builders of the Hall had thought about the dangers of a swollen river and how, without taking precautions, the island itself would one day disappear and so they built-up the island side of the riverbank in local stone by almost two feet so safeguarding 'Manger Isle' against further erosion and avoiding any possible flooding.

As the car turned around in the driveway Bailey's attention was caught by someone calling his name as they crunched down the driveway to his left. He turned to see a man dressed very formally in black with a gold waistcoat. He thought he might be something to do with funeral directors but then the man's expressionless face gave way to an almost imperceptible smile. 'You must be Police Constable Bailey, I presume?' Bailey nodded. 'Good afternoon to you sir. My name is Vaughton. I am Butler to his Lordship, Lord Manger, the master of the house.'

'Good afternoon Mr Vaughton, I'm PC Bailey though the PC isn't my -er no you already said that, didn't you? Well, in that case, just good afternoon!'

Vaughton remained impassive at Bailey's blundering attempt at an introduction and politely waited for him to finish. 'Please come this way, PC Bailey, his Lordship gave me strict instructions that you were to be brought to him as soon as you arrived.'

'Oh good, then lead on, sir.'

'It is Vaughton, sir, not sir'

Bailey looked quizzical but nodded all the same and indicated for the butler to lead the way and thought that the reason for the meeting was probably going to be to say hello. After all, his desk sergeant had been very clear that this was going to be a simple case of standing around and making some notes while a bunch of villagers stood up and talked. How difficult could that be? The Butler set off at a measured pace across the gravel and entered through the open front door, stopping for a moment to wipe his shoes on the matting, and waited while Bailey did the same and then continued onwards to a large six panel door leading off the inner hallway. He indicated to

Bailey to wait and then knocked softly, waited for a response and then entered the room, closing the door behind him. Bailey, left to his own devices for a few minutes, took the time to take in his surroundings; something he had always made a point of doing since he was a young boy. His father had told him that people often miss so much of where they are because they do not take the time to look around. He said, for example, that when you are in the High Street, always take the time to look up and you will be amazed at what you will see, as most people only look at the shop fronts and the doorways at street level and miss most of the detail and style that the Architects painstakingly incorporated into their designs. Therefore, Bailey had always made a point of looking up. Of course, this practice had a downside and, as a child, Bailey had spent so much time looking up that, that he had the odd misfortune and, in one particularly memorable incident, he knocked out his two front teeth because he failed to notice a lamp post until the very last moment. Luckily for him they were his milk teeth and over time they had been replaced with his adult teeth, though he had spent a couple of years with a very toothy grin, much to the amusement of his schoolmates. Bailey had never mastered whistling and he often wondered if that was why. As he had grown up there had also been a couple of near misses with a horse and cart and a coal truck and then, as a PC, he had bowled over an old couple as they made their way along the pavement but generally speaking, he maintained, his father's advice had been good and he was sure he had seen a lot more than the average person. Now, as he stood in the hallway, he looked up and around at the dark blue painted ceiling that had its own stars and sun. It was really very beautiful, he thought. In the centre was a glass dome through which could be seen patches of pale blue which were giving way to light grey clouds and the first hints of the storm to come. The inner hallway itself was an interesting eight-sided space with doors and corridors leading off in all directions. It reminded Bailey of the points of a compass and, when he glanced at the floor, he saw that the Architect must have been thinking of the same thing himself because there, picked out in blue, black and gold in the terrazzo floor was indeed the image of a very large compass. He also noticed that there was vase upon vase of red flowers everywhere he looked. It was a very impressive, if slightly repetitive, sight. The brass handle, polished to within an inch of its very existence, started to turn and Vaughton reappeared and beckoned him to enter. Once inside the room, Vaughton withdrew, closing the door behind him, instantly shutting out the hustle and bustle of the hallway and, briefly, there was only silence until his ears adjusted and tuned into the tick-tock of the grandfather clock that had marked the time in this study for over one hundred years.

'Ah, Bailey, good man! Please come in and sit down.' The voice was that of Marmaduke Manger who had risen from his seat at a large desk which faced the South wall, giving its occupant a view over well-kept lawns down to the river. A shadow passed outside as a member of staff crossed in front of the window carrying yet another pot of red flowers to somewhere. The east wall to the left of the desk was entirely taken up with a variety of dark wooden glass fronted cabinets and open shelves on, and in which, were an eclectic collection of animal heads, spears, rocks, bottles and pickling jars of all shapes and sizes, painted wooden faces, something with a lot of feathers, a musical instrument of some description and a bright red uniform. He stood up straight, pushing the wooden chair back with his knees, and placed his hands behind his back making no effort at all to welcome the Police Constable with a handshake.

'Thank you, Sir', replied Bailey, removing his helmet. Bailey perched on the nearest chair.

'I am Lord Manger, but I am sure that you were already aware of that.' He paused to receive an acknowledgement from Bailey who duly nodded before carrying on, 'now, do you know why you are here this afternoon, Bailey?'

'Yessir, my desk sergeant was clear about the money that has been left and the meeting that you are all having tonight to decide what to do with it.'

'Spot on. Good. Well, the fact is, Bailey, not everyone in the village is cock-a-hoop with some of the ideas that are being put forward. My idea needs to get the vote, naturally, and I expect you to ensure that any unruly elements are kept in their place. Do you understand me, Bailey?'

'I thought the idea was that there was going to be a vote?'

'Well of course there is, man, that's what the old girl wanted. But she wants the money to go for the good of the whole village, and the only way that is going to happen is for the money to come to me, man, don't you see?'

'I'm not sure that I do entirely sir, but I'm only here for the practice this afternoon; Police Constable Fogg will be attending the meeting proper tonight.'

Lord Manger's entire demeanour changed on realising his mistake, 'ah, I see. Well, in that case, Bailey, we don't need to discuss this any further. I will let you go about your duties. I will, um, discuss things further with your counterpart later. Do you know when he will be arriving?'

'At five o-clock this afternoon sir.' Bailey stood up and replaced his helmet. 'If there's nothing else sir....?'

'Just make sure that you bring Constable Fogg to see me as soon as he gets here.' As he spoke he turned away from Bailey and, as he passed, he picked up a crystal glass from his desk that contained the remainder of something which Bailey guessed from the colour was Whiskey. Lord Manger drained the dregs and absently gazed out of the window. The meeting was over and Bailey stood up and left the room, closing the door behind him, leaving his Lordship with his thoughts and the measured tick-tock from the clock. Standing back out in the hall, amongst the confusion, Bailey thought for a moment about that last image that he had of Marmaduke Manger standing at the window; something was wrong but he couldn't put his finger on what it was.

Chapter Six

Gino Vincenzi stood on the step and looked up at the skies, the clouds continued to present a solid front and coming over from across the moors there was evidence of darker skies approaching which, undoubtedly, meant more rain. Happy that he had selected the appropriate attire for the impending downpour, he pulled the side door closed and walked the short distance down the lane before turning into the High Street. He crossed over to the far side and before continuing his journey, he stopped to look back at his beloved restaurant. It was a sight that he knew he would never tire of; the double fronted bay windows and the full glass front door painted in white woodwork with bright yellow plinths below the windows and lace curtains gathered tightly together in the middle with pink bows, giving the appearance of two giant egg timers placed in the windows. Along the top of the frontage, picked out in, crisp white signwriting against a glossy black background, the words, 'La Bella Rose', the English translation being 'The Beautiful Rose'. He had opened for business almost two years ago and, for a small village, things had gone very well. He had quickly established a reputation as a dutiful and entertaining host, an excellent chef and, with many the ladies, an enthusiastic lover.

His latest conquest was the Lady of the Manor and, although he realised that he was sailing close to the wind with this relationship, because if Marmaduke were to find out, then he would be confronted with several problems, not least of which would be that Lord Manger was the landlord of his restaurant. He was fast coming to the conclusion that, although she was a good-looking woman, the consequences of this particular dalliance far outweighed the enjoyment and, he made another mental note that he must do something about it, sooner rather than later. He knew he could quite happily drop Buffy and move on to another, but he would kill before he gave up his precious 'La Bella Rose'.

He turned left and made his way along the tiny pavement passing 'Allens' the greengrocers, with its stall set to the side of the entrance door displaying an array of fruit and vegetables, and on past Halls' the cake shop, and then turning left past the 'Pig and Whistle' public house, where he could see the big shire horses that pulled the dray cart eating peacefully with their nosebags on whilst the draymen rolled the heavy wooden barrels off the back of the cart. He watched them as they dropped them onto a big hessian bag, preventing them from breaking, before skilfully wheeling the barrel around to line up with the skids on the cellar drop and, with a shout of 'all clear' to their unseen colleagues below, they would send the barrel on its way down and into the pub's cellar.

He walked on, taking the little lane that snaked up behind the row of cottages that faced the pub, and then in just another five minutes walking up the path as it climbed out of the village, until he stopped at the wooden stile. It was a good spot here to view the layout of the village and, also the geography of the surrounding land. It was easy to pick out the line of the river as it wound in a slow meander and formed the natural moat which had probably been the reason why Manger Hall had been constructed there in the first place, but the reason why Gino was now taking in this view was for the land, known as the South Woods, that lay beyond the river because that was the land that Gino had plans for; big plans that would indelibly stamp the name of Vincenzi on the map in this county - no, the country! If he was successful with his proposal tonight, then things were going to change around here and if that meant playing along with Buffy Manger for a little while longer, then it was a risk worth taking. He made another mental note to himself that, he would need to be a little less hasty in his severance plans, with the Lady of the Manor.

He unbuttoned his overcoat and checked his pocket watch; almost half past five. He had managed to slip away from the rehearsal earlier this afternoon, soon after the commotion had broken out following Marmaduke sitting on the nail. He had made the excuse of needing to sort out some preparations for Sunday lunch tomorrow but time was getting on and he was conscious he needed to get back to the Hall. The sky now an ominous dark grey, promised more heavy rain and, as he took the shortcut through the long, wet, grass of the lower meadow, he heard the first rumblings of thunder. He pulled up his collar and walked a little quicker. As he crossed the wooden footbridge, that provided the only other permanent access to the Manger Estate, he was taken aback for a moment at how swollen the river was. Something caught his attention and he looked up and saw a limp black wire overhead that had become snagged in the branches of a massive elm tree that overhung the river. He thought back to the remark he had overheard earlier from Buffy saying that the telephone was 'playing up', and he wondered if this was the reason. He was soon crunching across the gravel towards the rear of the house when he stopped and thought about what he was doing. He made the decision that, rather than come through the back like a servant, he would walk around the side of the house and come through the front so that everyone would notice him for the important figure in the community that he was. As he arrived at the front entrance he caught sight of a few the villagers, who were always early for everything, coming up the drive and he smiled inwardly to himself that he had made the right decision and outwardly to his possible supporters as he acknowledged them and moved into the entrance hall. He stood for a moment and thought that perhaps with the voting likely to be very tight, perhaps he should wait and welcome all of the early birds.

It was just as he stood half turned towards the front door, that he was nearly bowled over by the chambermaid as she burst out from the side corridor, her face completely ashen. He caught her by her shoulders, the young woman hardly noticed, her eyes were wild and she was looking past him. 'Steady on girl, you are in a one a big hurry. Is there something wrong?' Gino made an extra effort to speak with his best English accent because, he knew it would be important for the locals, to perceive him as one of their own, if he was going to get their vote tonight. Nevertheless, he couldn't help the odd extra 'a' sneaking into his vocabulary betraying his Italian origins.

The girl made no attempt at apologising for almost knocking him off his feet. 'Have you seen Mr Vaughton, sir, or her ladyship?' Her face showed her anxiety.

'No, I have only a just returned, I expect they are in the house somewhere, perhaps the Ballroom now that the people are arriving for the meeting. Is there something wrong, girl, answer me?'

'Oh dear, I need to find them, something terrible has happened and I was only a few minutes late. It wasn't my fault, I know it wasn't!' She was wringing her hands and looking about as if she was anticipating, perhaps foreseeing something bad happening to her in the near future. She looked scared to death.

'Slow down, just a slow down. You are not a making of the sense girl. What wasn't or isn't your fault?' Gino was still holding on to the girl just as a large party of villagers arrived through the front door to hear her exclaim.

'It's 'is Lordship, sir. He's dead!'

Chapter Seven

Had Gino Vincenzi spent a little more time looking over the South Woods, where he hoped his future lay with his proposed developments, he would have arrived at the footbridge a little later and, instead of taking in the majesty of the river as it surged under his feet, and at the telephone wire tangled in the branches, he would have seen instead, the great elm succumb to the combined effects of the recent persistent rain and the softening of the soil. He would have discovered that the reason for the tangled wire was not caused by the wind, as he had thought, but actually due to the shifting of the fifteen-ton trunk as it moved slowly, inexorably, sideways, gaining speed and then with a splintering, rending crash, toppling into the river taking with it, for good measure, a number of smaller trees, the telephone wire and most of the footbridge, leaving only a single rope suspended over the fast-flowing river. Indeed, had Mr Gino Vincenzi spent just a little more time pondering about his future, he might not have had one at all!

*

Gino helped the distraught chambermaid locate Mrs Manger who, as luck would have it, was talking to Vaughton at the time that they approached her. Buffy placed her hands in front of her mouth and stood frozen to the spot. Vaughton on the other hand, reacted immediately and, taking Buffy gently by the arm, led her to the staircase, pausing momentarily to stop a passing footman and whisper something to him, before continuing upstairs to the master bedroom, opening the door ahead of her and moving quickly to the bedside. Lord Manger was lying exactly as they had left him with his head propped up against the pillows; he looked to all intents and purposes as if he was sleeping but the muscles had the tell-tale relaxed look that only comes with death. Buffy touched the side of his face with her hand and immediately withdrew it as if it burnt but in fact it was her reaction to the already cooling skin. 'What should we do, Vaughton and where is that doctor?'

'I would respectfully suggest, madam, that we leave his Lordship until the doctor arrives. I am sure that he won't be much longer now.'

'Damn that drunk of a man; if he had gotten here sooner then perhaps dear Marm...Lord Manger might still be alive.'

'I am sure that the Doctor will be able to ascertain that, madam.' Vaughton paused and cleared his throat, as if he was hesitating.

Buffy looked up from her dead husband and sensed his apprehension. 'What is it, Vaughton?'

'I was wondering, madam, if we should leave things just as they are and- and ask the Police Constable to join us?'

'Vaughton, as we do have a Police Constable at the Hall now, I am sure that he will want to come up and see for himself my dear husband, but that isn't what you are saying is it? You think someone has done him in, don't you!'

'I wouldn't have put it quite like that, but Lord Manger was quite well until his accident with the chair and now he is dead. I just wondered if it would be opportune, madam, nothing more.'

She shot him a glance and met his steely eyes looking straight into hers. 'You're right, of course, Vaughton. Will you please arrange for Constable Bailey to come up?'

'I had already anticipated your agreement and sent that footman to find him before we came up, Madam. I expect that is him coming along the landing now.'

'Well!' Lady Manger looked incredulous, but her butler remained impassive and looked towards the bedroom door, where, a moment later, the figure of PC Bailey loomed large.

'I was just acquainting myself with the kitchen staff when this chap came and said you wanted me up here as quickly as possible. I couldn't think what it might be but on the way through the house, I heard two of the staff saying that his Lordship had died. That can't be, can it?'

The two figures stood motionless at the bedside as he approached and so he made his way along the opposite side of the bed in order that he could have a good look himself at Lord Manger. He leaned over and turned his head sideways and listened for any signs of breathing but there was nothing. He placed the back of his hand against the man's cheek and he, too, felt the coolness of the skin. His career in the police force had led him to examine a few dead people over the years and he was satisfied that Lord Manger was another one to add to his list. 'We will have to wait for the doctor to confirm things, of course, but I am fairly sure that Mr Manger has passed on. I am very sorry, Mrs Manger, I realise this must all have come as a bit of a shock.'

Buffy put her hands to her face and turned away from her husband's body and, brushing past Vaughton, she walked hurriedly from the room. She was making odd little noises, supposedly of distress, thought Bailey. As she made it to the door, she lowered her hands and blurted out to the two men, 'I'm sorry, you must excuse me, this really couldn't have come at a worse time. I must go and prepare for the meeting.' And then she was gone. Bailey looked at the empty doorway and assumed he heard the Lady of the Manor, fighting to hold back her real emotions until she was alone, as she hurried away along and around the landing. He heard a door open and close and then the only sounds coming in through the doorway were those of the general hubbub from the hallway below.

'Mr Vaughton. I think it would be sensible if we leave this room as it is and I will wait outside of the door until the doctor gets here.'

'Just as you wish, Constable.' With that, the butler moved silently, in the way that only butlers can, to the door and, with a slight cough indicated to the Constable that he would wait for him to leave his erstwhile employer's bedroom together. He was, after all, still the butler of this household, at least for the time being. Bailey took one last look at the expressionless face of Marmaduke Manger and, satisfied that he was indeed dead, joined Vaughton at the door where they both stepped out on to the polished wood floor of the landing and the butler drew the door closed behind him. Bailey took up a position in front of the doors with his hands behind his back in what he imagined was how a guard would stand and looked sternly forward. As the butler moved away to the top of the stairs a thought suddenly burst into the policeman's thoughts. 'Oh, Mr Vaughton, I've just thought of something. I don't suppose there are any other ways to get into this room are there?'

'There is an adjoining door to her Ladyship's rooms but...' Vaughton broke off as if he was considering if he should continue with the conversation. He arrived at a decision and continued, 'the connecting door has a wardrobe in front of it on both sides, the door itself is locked and the whereabouts of the only key is unclear. In short, PC Bailey, let us say that there has been little need for urgent communication between the two rooms for some time.' Vaughton paused again and then added, 'there is also a balcony, but I doubt anyone would attempt to enter or leave by that method, so I would say that you stand at the only entrance. Does that clarify things constable Bailey?'

'It does, Mr Vaughton, thank you.'

From his position, PC Bailey could see through the balusters down into the hallway. A lot of people were milling around who he assumed must be the invited guests for the meeting this evening. From what he could see and overhear, they were a real mixture. Most looked as if they were working folk; their clothes mainly brown and worn with voices that were difficult to hear clearly as individuals, whereas there was a smaller group who stood together with much finer clothes of brighter colours and from time to time, he could hear shrieks and guffaws of laughter from these people but somehow it all seemed false as if they were trying to laugh at each other but it didn't sound real. He thought to himself how you sometimes got a better idea of people if you looked at them from a distance but then decided that didn't really work because you couldn't see or hear them clearly. Three more thoughts came into his mind, almost together. First, he wondered how long the doctor was going to take to arrive. Second, his conversation with the cook had been interrupted by the turn of events, with his Lordship passing away so suddenly, but he was sure that it was carrot cake that he was about to be offered. Third, what on earth could have caused his Lordship to have died so suddenly?

He didn't have long to wait for the answer to his first question as a thickset man in his forties appeared at the top of the stairs. He was carrying a large leather bag in his left hand and an overcoat that had clearly seen recent use was draped over his right arm as he advanced towards the bedroom door and the police constable. His skin was almost the colour of milk, which was in stark contrast to his shock of red hair and his slightly wild full beard 'You must be Bailey. I'm David Macdonald, Doctor David Macdonald.' The figure said in a very well-educated accent with just a trace of his Highlands origins. Bailey brightened a little. 'They told me downstairs to come straight up. Shall we go in?' With a smart side-stepping motion Bailey opened the door and the doctor swept past him into the bedroom. He followed him, closing the door and turning the key in the lock, ensuring that the examination of the dead man would be made without interruption. 'So, Bailey, perhaps you can fill me in with the details of what happened here this afternoon', he said, while draping his overcoat over the end of the bed and then doing likewise with his jacket. He rolled up his shirt sleeves and, with no more than a cursory look at his face, took the edge of the bedspread and pulled it back, exposing the body of Marmaduke Manger to the waist. Bailey was taken aback at the sudden exposure of the man who had held such command of the conversation that they had had just a few short hours ago. He was still dressed in his shirt and trousers but he hadn't expected to see so much of a dead body in one go. He noticed the doctor was looking at him while he laid his hands on the corpse, pushing and prodding here and there. 'Well, man, what have you to tell me?'

'Sorry, I was just staring there for a minute. Now, let me think. Well, I'm not from here.'

'I know that already. I am the local GP, if you remember, so I have a pretty good idea of who lives in the village.'

'Yes, of course you do. Sorry. Well you also probably know about the big meeting here tonight to decide what to do with the money?' A nod confirmed he did. 'So, at the rehearsal this afternoon, I was standing at the far end of the ballroom, just looking really. The people who are going to make a speech, that's - er one moment.' Bailey took out his notebook from his top pocket and thumbed through a few pages before finding what he was looking for. 'Yes, here we go. Lord Manger is going, or *was,* perhaps I should say, to speak first and then the Vicar Reverend Smeeton. After him it was supposed to be Kate Rimehill the Maid and then Mr Gino Vincenzi, he's Italian, and then the voting was going to start.' Satisfied that he had taken down the information correctly, he closed his notebook and continued. 'The other speeches didn't happen because after Mr Manger finished his, he sat down and jumped straight back up, yelling at the top of his voice and grabbing hold of his behind. The noise he was making was unbelievable, nobody was sure what was going on, there was just this shouting coming from his Lordship who started rolling around on the floor. People started trying to help him and see what was wrong, then Mr Vaughton took charge and Mrs Manger came into the room with a young man. She seemed to have better luck calming his Lordship down and, after a while, she organised with the butler to have him moved up here, saying that he would be more comfortable.

'I see. Well let's have a look, then shall we?' the doctor made an initial visual examination of the body then, from time to time, he stopped and put his stethoscope and tapped an area or rubbed the skin, once or twice he lifted up a limb. Sometimes he did the action more than once. His actions were accompanied by noises, perhaps 'mmm', or 'aha', or 'yes' and on two occasions an 'oh, dear me'. After ten minutes or so the doctor turned to Bailey with a worried expression and called him over to join him at the bedside. 'Look here Bailey, what do you see around the outside of the body on the bedsheet?'

Bailey looked in the general direction that the doctor pointed in but couldn't really see anything at all 'umm I'm not sure, sir.'

'Take a closer look, man, there, right next to the body. Get closer and tell me what you see.'

Bailey moved closer so that his face and, particularly his nose, was much closer to the body than he would have wanted to be out of choice but, in doing so, he did see something. 'There seems to be a line, like a tide-mark in the bath sir, it follows all along the body.'

'Brilliant, well done, Bailey, exactly right. There is a mark. It's sweat. Lord Manger was clearly sweating like a horse pulling a coal cart and yet someone tucked him up tightly in bed.'

'I understand from Mr Vaughton that it was Mrs Manger that took charge of his Lordship once he had been carried to the bed. She had also arranged for the maid to pop in on Lord Manger every hour just to make sure that he was alright. It was the maid that discovered him; when she made her first visit she realised something was wrong and came downstairs to tell everyone. I must admit, sir, when I came into the room and looked at the body, I thought then that he looked a bit pink, like he was hot, but that didn't make any sense to me because, of course, he wasn't even warm when I touched him.'

'There's a reason for that, Bailey, and look here, look at those ankles, look at how puffy they are.'

'Is that because he got hot as well?' quizzed Bailey surveying the ankles and the well-manicured toes, that he noted, were now a distinctly grey colour.

'No, I don't think so. The fact is, constable, that I have concluded my preliminary investigation and though I am willing to stand corrected if the laboratory results show otherwise, I believe this man was poisoned.'

'Poisoned! But what with, sir, and how?'

'It's interesting and I haven't quite got the answer yet. I would really like to go down and have a look at that chair for myself but, from what you have told me, and considering how quickly his condition changed, it must have happened when he sat down.'

'Right, sir. The chair must still be down in the ballroom, so we can go and have a look right away. You didn't mention what he was poisoned with, but perhaps you'll know after we look at that chair? If you're ready, let's get going. I'll lock the door behind us.'

Bailey was looking out for Vaughton as he came back down the staircase but he couldn't see him amongst the crowd of villagers filing into the ballroom. He made a sharp turn to the right, taking him and the doctor, who was following closely behind, along a service corridor which came out to the side of the kitchen. He prided himself of always making a point to find out the whereabouts of any refreshments very early on in his investigations and Manger Hall was no exception. He called to a young man in the scullery. 'Do you know where I might find Mr Vaughton?' The young man indicated with his hand that he was through the doorway to the left and then disappeared on his way. Bailey opened the door and strode on around the corner, almost colliding with his quarry, who was holding open the door to the cheese pantry, giving instructions to a young serving maid. He looked up, startled and slightly annoyed by the high-speed intrusion of the constable.

'Is there something I can do for you, Constable Bailey?'

'Indeed, there is, sir. Me and the doctor here,' Bailey jerked his head in the direction of the bearded face peering over his shoulder, 'we need to take a look at the chair with the nail in it, the one that Lord Manger wishes he hadn't sat on. Is it still in the ballroom, Mr Vaughton?'

Vaughton dismissed the maid who turned to the two gentlemen now standing behind her and gave a small curtsey before scurrying off along the corridor. Vaughton closed the storeroom door and locked it from a bunch of keys that he was holding in his right hand. He turned and peered down his nose at the policeman and his medical sidekick. 'I removed the offending chair from the Ballroom as soon as I returned from carrying his Lordship to his bedroom. I wasn't going to risk anyone else sitting on it.'

Bailey looked crestfallen for a moment but, before he could say anything, the butler continued. 'However, I wanted to hold on to the evidence because I planned to discuss the poor repair work that Clott had carried out on it with him later, so I placed it in the wood store. Please follow me.' With that, he strode past the pair and opened a door that led into a small porch with slit windows in either side. There was a set of shelves under the left-hand window on which stood a number of lamps and boxes of matches. Vaughton shook a couple of lamps and happy that they contained sufficient oil, lifted the glasses on them and took a match from the box and lit both wicks. The creamy yellow light grew as the flame fanned out along the edge of the wick. He closed the glasses once more, which increased the light still further. The air was filled with a combination of the sulphur from the match and the smell of the paraffin oil. 'If you don't mind, PC Bailey, will you take one of these?'

'Of course, sir.' Vaughton signalled to the two of them the availability of several umbrellas in a stand and then, opening the outer door, stepped out into the pouring rain. Bailey didn't bother with an umbrella and the doctor caught up with Vaughton and shared his as the threesome made the short walk across to the outbuildings. Vaughton flicked through the keys in his hand and selected one, but stopped before he inserted it into the keyhole.

'Look at this,' he said holding up the lamp and pointing to the door in front of him. 'Someone has attempted to force the door open. Why in heaven's name would anyone try to do that?' Bailey and the Doctor exchanged glances, Vaughton caught the exchange and gave the two men an enquiring look. 'It seems gentleman, that you might be able to shed some more light on what is going on here and, I do not mean from the lamp you are holding?'

'Not at all sir, perhaps someone couldn't find the key and needed something urgently.' The butler's face showed that he wasn't convinced by the constable's response but he could see that no further explanation was forthcoming, so he proceeded to unlock the door. The heavy door swung slowly open, and it was easy to see a number of deep depressions in the doorframe where a heavy bar or object of some description had been used unsuccessfully to lever open the door. Vaughton ran his hand up and down the frame.

'Someone really wanted to get in here, perhaps we disturbed them, quite extraordinary, and there isn't anything in here of any value' He glanced from the face of the policeman to the doctor and back again, but once again, neither of them gave away their thoughts. It was dark in the store and the light from the lamps accentuated just how dark it had become outside, although it was still early afternoon, and all three men in the party shuffled forwards like moths around a flame. The room was packed with all manner of things. Vaughton had referred to the room as 'the wood store' and, indeed, there was an ample quantity of timber stacked neatly against the side wall, but there was also some crude racking along the back of the room which contained flower pots, a scythe blade caked in rust, a number of lengths of rope, a pile of hessian sacks in one corner, and there, right in the middle of the floor, sat a very sturdy high back wooden chair, totally incongruous with its surroundings, because only hours before it had graced the ballroom and, as such, was well polished and cared for, while the majority of the things in this room bore out the Butler's earlier question of why would anyone want to break in. Bailey inspected the chair and, at first glance, the gold coloured cushion appeared intact. However, when he depressed it with his hand the dull point of the nail showed through. The doctor shifted around to the side of the chair and looked closely at the nail.

'Be careful, Bailey, not to touch that point.' Dr Macdonald produced a small pen knife from his pocket and gently scraped at the nail. Small flakes came off on to the blade. The doctor examined them under the light and then carefully wiped the knife in his handkerchief, making sure all of the flakes remained in the cloth as he folded it over into a neat parcel before placing it into his inside jacket pocket. 'Thank you, Vaughton, that's all I need for now but I would ask you if the constable might take possession of that key. I may need to examine that chair again.'

'Very good, Doctor, just as you wish.' The party returned into the house, thankful to get out of the rain. The policeman and doctor made their excuses and left Vaughton to cogitate over what had occurred out there in his storeroom while they made their way to the inner hallway. Bailey opened the door to the study and was surprised to notice how the door dragged on the threshold. He hadn't noticed it when Vaughton had closed the door earlier. Apart from that, the room looked just as before, although the spring sunlight that had flooded through the window where Bailey had left Marmaduke Manger alive and well earlier that morning had now been replaced by heavy rain lashing against the glass.

'Well Doctor Macdonald, what do you think now?'

The doctor collected his thoughts for a moment before answering, as he understood that what he was about to say to the constable, seemed incongruous to everything that he knew about the people in this tiny community of West Mucklington Parva. He joked whenever he met up with medical colleagues who asked him where his practice was located, that the name of the village was longer than the village itself! Nevertheless, he was a factual man and so steeled himself to deliver his opinion, based on what he had seen with his own eyes. 'I am sorry to have to inform you Bailey that from what I have seen from the condition of the body and, the fact that the nail was definitely coated with something, although I won't know exactly what with until I get it analysed, the evidence compels me to arrive at the conclusion', he took a deep breath. 'That Lord Manger was poisoned by whatever is on that nail.'

'But if you're right, sir, then that would mean that someone is putting poison nails in chairs, which is a daft thing to do because people are going to sit on them and get hurt!'

'That's exactly my point, Bailey, though, if you pardon the pun, that isn't the point.' An expectant look came back from the law officer's face, but nothing more. The doctor decided to press on, as the explanation would probably take far too long. 'I don't think someone is putting poison nails *per se* in lots of chairs, I think they just put one nail in that one particular chair.'

'Right, sir, that's very helpful. I really couldn't have arrived at who put the nail in the chair any quicker than you have. My plan, sir, is now to wait for my relief, Police Constable Fogg to arrive, and then I will set about tackling this Percy chap if you just point him out before you get off back to your surgery.'

'PC Bailey, what are you talking about?'

'This chap, Percy, who put the nail in the chair.'

'I didn't say that at all.'

'Yes, you did, sir; you said someone called Percy put one nail in one chair.'

'No Bailey, what I said was *'per se',* it's Latin for 'as such'. So what I mean is that I don't think someone is putting nails all over the place in lots of chairs, otherwise everyone would have sat on one, but clearly they meant to put one in the chair that Lord Manger would sit on. Do you see what I mean now?'

'Right, sir, I have it now.' Bailey stopped and thought for a moment and then, as if a light even brighter than the lamp in the storeroom that contrasted so starkly had suddenly come on said, 'crikey, sir, but, if you're right about that nail being poisoned, and the fact that his Lordship is dead does go a long way to backing you up, then that means that someone, probably not called Percy, put that nail in the chair on purpose to kill his Lordship. But that's murder!'

'Yes constable, I realise what I am suggesting, but look here, I may be mistaken, I don't have solid proof yet about what is on that nail. I don't think we should be too hasty.' But Bailey wasn't listening to the doctor anymore; he was lost in his own thoughts as one realisation crashed into another. Here he was again at a simple village meeting, not even the meeting in fact, just the rehearsal, and someone had been murdered. Here he was, PC Bailey on his own again, with a good chance the murderer was still here walking around, perhaps they would strike again. Here he was, yet again, without a single clue who he was looking for or why they had done it. He could feel the panic rising in his chest but then he thought about how proud his lovely wife Sarah and his children had looked when he had been praised by the Chief Constable of Devon for helping solve the murders at Lewtrenchard Manor last year. He remembered looking across and seeing the joy in her beautiful green eyes and how his children had run into his arms and told him that he was a hero. He didn't really think that he was but it was a good feeling all the same. And then that feeling became a memory once again as the panic returned but, as he looked at the doctor looking at him, he thought that this time things would be different because, this time, he had PC Fogg coming to help him and the doctor was returning to the village in a moment and hopefully he could telephone from his own surgery and speak to his desk sergeant and send more men up from Exeter and everything would turn out alright. Yes, he felt better already!

'Bailey, are you alright?'

'Oh, yes, Doctor Macdonald, I'm fine. Now, let's get you on your way. When you arrive at your surgery, I want you to telephone Heavitree Police Station in Exeter and ask for the desk sergeant and tell him everything that we have talked about and ask him to send some more men up with PC Fogg. I know you won't have the results of those flakes you took just yet, but at least we can take some people in for questioning about what they saw and the like and then, if what you think has happened, really happened, then we might already be halfway to catching the killer, before he or she even realises that we are on to 'em.'

'I certainly will do so, constable, and, as it turns out, I can carry out some preliminary tests back at my practice and, if it the substance on the nail, is what I think it is, then I will be able to come back to you with a fairly positive result.' With that, the doctor opened his medical bag and removed a small jar. He then took the handkerchief from his inside jacket pocket and pushed it carefully into the jar, sealing it with a cork before placing it, along with its valuable contents, in his bag. He snapped the bag shut and buttoned up his overcoat as he and the constable made their way out of the front entrance and walked in silence down the gravelled drive, both men lost in their own thoughts about the events that had taken place at Manger Hall. PC Bailey walked with the doctor as far as the stone bridge.

'I'll leave you here, doctor, and get back to the house. I already know who put the nail in the chair and I need to keep a close eye on him.' He bid the doctor goodbye and set off back across the drive. He was halfway back when he heard the shout and turned to see Doctor Macdonald crouching on the bridge as if he was caught off balance. There was curious, yet wild, look in his eyes and he was peering at the parapet of the bridge. PC Bailey followed his gaze and at first saw nothing unusual but then, almost in slow motion he saw the topmost stone of the parapet tumble into the fast-flowing river, then another stone and then two more. He looked back with a quizzical look at the doctor, not really understanding what it was that he was looking at.

*

The elm had easily smashed through the rope footbridge and had managed to lose most of its larger boughs as it fell into the river. The main trunk, tangled up with the wreckage of the footbridge had spun slowly this way and that, completely at the whim of the water, before becoming snagged on the inner bank of the meander as it made its way down the river. This tangle was soon joined with other debris and, in a short time, the growing mass formed a makeshift dam, trying to hold back the surging waters. Smaller trees and clumps of grass, broken off from the banks, continued to back-up behind this haphazard structure, the relentless pressure of the river increased until, finally, as a now sizeable blockage, it broke away from the bank and slewed out of the meander and into the section of the swollen river that passed along the front of Manger Hall. Having finally won the battle the swirling current, broke the dam into pieces, forcing the largest section containing the trunk of the elm to forge ahead on its own mini tidal wave. The old stone bridge had served the Manger estate well and had carried foot traffic and horses and carts for many a long year and later the carts had been replaced by cars and lorries all of which the sturdy structure had taken in its stride. But the combination of those years of faithful service, the surcharge of an unnaturally high river and the sudden impact in the centre of the span by the elm tree that now more resembled a battering ram, had proven to be the proverbial straw on the camel's back. The impact cracked the bridge clean through at precisely the time that the Scotsman, on his mission to prove there was a murder afoot, and on his way to organise reinforcements for the lone policeman, had made it to the apex, too far to run in either direction to save himself. The bridge shuddered, throwing him off balance and all he could do was observe the rapid disintegration of the *terra firma* underneath him as it, and him, disappeared into the murky waters leaving a thirty-foot-wide gap where just seconds before it had stood.

Bailey rushed to the river's edge hoping he might find the doctor clinging to the bank but there was nothing left, just swirling water, and the odd 'sploosh' as more masonry fell into the river. He ran along the bank, calling out for the doctor, until his progress was blocked by overhanging bushes, but there was not a trace of the bridge, the elm tree or any reply from Doctor Macdonald. He walked back to where the bridge had stood, constantly checking the river for any sign but when he looked across the gaping hole, he realised that there was no way that anyone would be coming across that way to join him tonight. He trudged back to the house; there didn't seem like there was anything else to do. He would organise a search party, of course, in the vain hope that the doctor still might be clinging on to a branch or something but, as the river curved away from the estate soon after the bridge and, as no one could get off the island, he didn't see there would be much prospect of that happening. His hopes soared for a few brief moments when one of the footmen informed him that there was a smaller footbridge at the rear of the estate but, when the report came back that that bridge had suffered the same fate, his hopes were dashed once more. As he sat and thought about his predicament, he couldn't imagine what his desk sergeant would say; he wouldn't believe a word of it!

Chapter Eight

'Oh, I'm sorry, PC Bailey, I didn't realise that anyone would be using this room.'

'You mean, with his Lordship being dead and all, Reverend Smeeton?'

'No, I rather meant, well, I don't know what I meant, really. Anyway, I was just making the most of the peace and quiet that one is afforded in here to finish off my sermon.'

'Don't mind me, your reverendship, I was just coming in to take a look around at things in general. No real reason, you understand, just out of interest like.' PC Bailey winced at his weak explanation for having come into Lord Manger's study for the second time without any permission. The fact was, he wanted to examine the items on the shelves in the hope of finding a bottle of poison. He wasn't entirely sure what he was going to do if he found one, but at least it was a start to his investigation. He wanted Smeeton to leave because, otherwise, he suspected the inquisitive vicar would start asking difficult questions that he wasn't in a position to answer.

'I see, constable. Does your desire to look around have any connection with the death of Lord Manger?'

The first difficult question already, thought Bailey. He tried to deflect it. 'Mr Smeeton, it is actually very fortunate for me that you are in here. You see I think I have asked everyone else who was in the ballroom at the time that Lord Manger had his unfortunate accident. I made a mental note of who was there and drew up a list and you are the last name on it. I wonder if you would be so good as to tell me what you saw from, say, half an hour before the incident.'

'Of course, PC Bailey, a simple task actually. I had walked over from St Julian's and arrived here around noon, perhaps a little after, as I think I recall hearing the bell in the clock tower chiming as I came over the bridge. I was welcomed by Lord Manger himself who spotted me coming up the drive. He mentioned that he wanted to talk to me about a couple of pressing matters and that one of them was to do with the money that Rose had bequeathed to the village. I mentioned that I could come and talk to him straight after the rehearsal, at which he became agitated, I have no idea why. He asked if I could make it any sooner and I said "no", that wouldn't be possible because I was meeting Lady Manger in the drawing room to go over the music for the ceremony at the end of the month at St Julian's where we would celebrate the generosity of Rose Stimper in song. I recall that he made a comment about his wife knowing more about spaghetti than she did about music which, I thought at the time, was odd but didn't give it another thought. Lord Manger then agreed to meet me in here immediately after the rehearsal and asked me not to mention that we were going to meet to anyone else, especially his wife or Mr Vincenzi. I agreed and we went our separate ways. He strode off muttering something about his toes were pinching in his riding boots because Harry Clott had ruined his favourite ones and that he was going to have to do something about that boy once and for all. I went on my way to the drawing room and, as I passed the ballroom, Lady Manger was just coming out; we almost bumped into each other. She was very on edge during our meeting; her mind really wasn't focussed on the selection of the musical pieces at all. I think I could have suggested anything and she would have agreed, she really was very preoccupied. Anyway, she made her excuses and left me saying she had to finish off the flower arrangements and so I went into the ballroom and waited for everyone else to arrive.'

'I see sir, thank you, and do you remember anyone else coming into the ballroom while you sat there and waited?'

'Let me see. I think that someone did come in, was it Vaughton or Harry? Do you know, I can't quite recall? I'm sorry, PC Bailey, I will have to give it some thought, would that be alright?'

'Yes of course, your reverendship. There are a number of loose ends, though, and things I still need to talk to everyone about who was on my list, so perhaps you can let me know later what you saw. As I say, I made up the list out of my head from whom I think I remembered being there at the time. I wonder if you could help me by checking the names to make sure that I have included everyone?'

'Of course, can I ask what else you need to know?' replied Smeeton looking over the top of his gold rimmed glasses.

Second difficult question!

'Erm, yes, of course. I didn't ask where everyone was standing at the time of the speech, stupid really, but it has occurred to me since that there is a possibility the chair Lord Manger sat on could have been sat on by him by mistake.' Bailey breathed a sigh of relief and felt quite pleased with himself, because when he started the reply he didn't think that what he was going to say was relevant at all, but now he had said what he said, it suddenly dawned on him that, in fact, it was very important, as there was always the possibility that the intended victim had not been Lord Manger at all.

The vicar eyed him suspiciously but asked nothing further. 'I have a pen and some spare paper from my sermon notes so I'll jot down the names here and see if it is the same as the names you have on your list, that way I won't have been influenced by who you thought was there. How about that, PC Bailey, for an idea?' The constable nodded in agreement, it was a very good idea and not one that he would have readily thought of. 'Now, let me see. There was Lord Manger and myself, of course, Mr Vincenzi, the maid, Kate, Mr Vaughton joined us once the speech had begun, oh - and Harry, not forgetting Mrs Manger and you, PC Bailey.'

'Thank you, sir. I think it is safe to rule me out...'

'Rule you out...of what, constable?'

'Of putting a nail in the chair, I had only just arrived after all, and had no knowledge of anyone here. On top of that, sir, I am a policeman, so I wouldn't do it would I?'

'In these troubled times, with all the terrible things that we hear going on in Europe, PC Bailey, we cannot be sure about anyone, can we? What are you going to do with the information, constable? I mean, it is hardly a crime is it, unless you are suggesting that the nail had something to do with his Lordship's death? The vicar caught the expression on his face. 'I say, you think it might have done, don't you? Was it the shock of the nail, or was it something else, something more sinister?'

'Thank you, Mr Smeeton, for the information. I would like to address all of those people on your list, I don't think there is any need to have the conversation in front of the rest of the villagers. I wonder if you would be good enough to go and find Mr Vaughton and ask him to gather those people together in the dining room?'

Reverend Smeeton was still looking for an answer to his supposition but could see that nothing was forthcoming from Bailey and so succumbed to his request, taking up his notes and moving to the door. 'Very well, Bailey, I will do as you ask. Shall we say ten minutes time in the dining room, then?'

'Yes, thank you, sir, that will be most helpful.' Bailey avoided the gaze of the reverend. He had learned over the years to avoid as many questions as possible, from listening to people avoiding his questions, but he felt bad about not being truthful with a man of the cloth. But the fact remained that Reverend Smeeton's name was on the list and that, however unlikely it might seem, he had to assume that he might just as easily be the poisoner as anyone else.

Once the vicar had left the room, Bailey set about looking at the various oddities that he assumed Lord Manger had collected on his travels around the world. He found the assortment of jars, but none of them had the word 'Poison' in bold letters on the front or even a skull and crossbones; instead they had things crammed into them with some sort of clear liquid around them. They reminded him of the jars of pickles he saw in his mother's pantry when he was a small boy. His mother was an avid pickler. He picked up a jar and turned it in his hand to study the label more closely which had some words handwritten in a flowery script, quite faded now over the years, which read, *Romaleidae Agriacris Magnifica.* The creature inside didn't look anywhere near as grand as the label said, it looked like a big grasshopper, while in another, was some sort of worm with a lot of legs called a *Diplopoda.* He wasn't enjoying picking up the jars, though he was sure that the creatures must be dead. In two of the larger ones, he discovered what looked like mice but they didn't have a label on them and, he was most definitely not going to open the lid for a closer inspection. He looked further along the shelf and, behind the blade of the spear he had noticed when he had met Lord Manger earlier, he found an ancient cricket ball and, further along, a picture of what must have been Lord Manger with a young woman on his arm. The picture was faded and taken some years before, but the features of the recently deceased Earl were clear to see, unless it was his brother or even his father, perhaps. He reached the end of the last shelf and sighed to himself. The search had been interesting but there was no poison. He returned to the desk and sat down looking out of the window, wondering what his next move should be. Nothing was coming to mind, but then that was a feeling Bailey often had. He wondered if he should just ask them all, if one of them had poisoned the man. He had had some success in the past with this direct questioning technique, but he wasn't sure if he could try it in a group situation. Whilst he sat there, he casually twirled his fingers around the heavy paperweight that sat on top of the pile of papers in the middle of the desk. He didn't remember them being there earlier in the day. The vicar had said he had been writing his sermon notes and so he assumed he must have inadvertently left them behind when he left the room. Bailey casually slid the polished brass elephant figurine to one side and glanced over the letter. He was surprised to see that it wasn't addressed to the vicar at all but was some correspondence to Lord Manger requesting permission to organise a shoot on his land later in the year. He read the letter again and then thought that perhaps the vicar was going to announce it in his sermon. He put the letter to one side and checked the next. It too was addressed to his Lordship and concerned some matters to do with the South woods. There was a note written across the top in green ink which read '*7:30, White Horse Club, Pall Mall*'. Bailey had no idea who had written the comment or who 'Pall Mall' might be, but he took out his own note book and jotted it down all the same. He continued through the pile, all the paperwork was addressed to Lord Manger and he was still puzzling over why the vicar would have had these papers, when he came across two sheets folded over at ninety degrees to the rest of the pile. He slid them out, unfolded them and read the first which had the bold heading;

HATTENSCHWELLER HIGH SCHOOL
BRIGHTON

He read on;

12th August 1916

Dear Sir,

With regard to the matter of the young person that you have placed in our care. I am pleased to report a successful settling period has now been completed.

As discussed, there will be no further need for you to contact this establishment on any issue regarding the child's welfare.

I trust that, for your part, we can rely on prompt payment of our fees, if this arrangement is to continue.

Yours sincerely,

Helga Hattenschweller

Headmistress & Hockey Captain

He thought the second sheet might be a continuation of the first but when he saw the crest at the top of the page, he thought again.

Centurian de Fleur

- Money Matters ~ It really does ~

20th January '38

Dear Lord Manger,

It gives me no comfort to inform you that we find your latest proposals for repayment to be somewhat dubious.

However, considering your previous dealings, we are willing to give you the benefit of the doubt, as you assure us you will be receiving a substantial amount from the Stimper estate.

We will to hold off repayment of your loan of £75,000.00 until after the forthcoming 'General Meeting'. We trust everything turns out as expected, otherwise we may have to consider how to recover our monies.

With deepest sincerity,

Mortlake Segrue

The Loan Arranger

He read through the two letters three times, each in the hope that he would be able to make sense of what he was reading. There was a definite mention of a child at a school, though he was sure that he had heard no mention from anyone that there was a child and, on checking the date and counting backwards, he realised that the letter had been written twenty-two years ago, so the child wouldn't really be a child anymore and that would explain why they weren't here as a child, if indeed, they were here at all. The second letter was clearly much more recent. He folded the two letters together, failing to notice that the folds fitted so well together, as if they had been folded at the same time and yet they were over twenty years apart. He placed the elephant back on guard of the remaining papers, stood up from the desk and made his way to the dining room, where he hoped the vicar had been successful in rounding up the group of people that he needed to ask some further questions.

Apart from the location of the Kitchen, Bailey wasn't completely *au fait* with the layout of Manger Hall and, as he didn't want to have to walk through the ballroom, from where he could hear the general hubbub of the villagers probably discussing the fate of the Lord of the Manor, he took a tortuous route from the inner hall, turning right and then left along a corridor which was adorned with portrait after portrait of various stern looking gentlemen in various poses. He noted, that the most popular pose, appeared to be sitting on a horse or sitting upright with hands clasped over the arms of a very grandiose gilt chair with dogs lying at their feet. There was one young man in a white uniform with a gun over one shoulder and a lion's skin draped over the other which at first glance, made him look as if he had two heads. 'Horace Tarquin Manger – Big Game Hunter', Bailey read on the small brass plaque at the bottom of the painting. He walked on around the corner but slowed as he heard raised voices up ahead. The corridor changed dramatically half way along to the right where it widened out to become the inner glazed wall of a conservatory or, perhaps an orangery. Bailey neither knew nor cared which it was, but he was interested to see the Italian man, Mr Vincenzi, and Mrs Manger standing facing each other. She was dressed in a white full-length dress that only someone with a figure like hers could get away with, and she certainly did; she wore a single red flower just below her left shoulder which, set off the outfit to great effect. As Bailey stood and watched this scene, he thought how fortunate Mrs Manger had been to wear a dress with a flower, that matched the red flowers evident all over the Manor House this evening...

Buffy stood with her hands by her side but they were clenching and unclenching, making fists as if perhaps she was about to strike the man. Mr Vincenzi, dressed in an immaculately cut black silk dinner suit, was busy gesturing with his hands and arms making staccato jabs in the space between them. Bailey had met a few Italian people before on his beat in Exeter, and it had always struck him that they were a race of people who liked to talk with their hands. He mentioned it to his sergeant in conversation, who replied, 'I know what you mean, Bailey; I reckon that if you cut off their hands they wouldn't be able to talk at all.' He had never really understood that comment until now. The sound of the rain drumming on the glass roof made it impossible to make out what either person was saying, but it was clear from his actions that he was defending his point of view. He saw that the Italian gentleman was holding a piece of paper in his right hand and kept hitting it with the back of his left hand as if he was constantly referring to it. As Bailey moved into the peripheral vision of Mrs Manger, she snapped her head around to see who it was and gave a visible jolt at the sight of the advancing police constable.

'PC Bailey,' she said, struggling for what to say next. 'I, I was just informing Mr Vincenzi here, that we need to assemble in the dining room as you have something to say to us all ahead of the village meeting. Isn't that right, Mr Vincenzi?'

Gino Vincenzi relaxed his shoulders and wiped his hand down his face, visibly changing his demeanour as he did it. He quickly folded the sheet of paper and put it away inside his jacket. He shrugged and gestured with an upturned hand in the direction of Lady Manger, 'yes indeed, PC Bailey, the lady, she is correct in what she says. Shall we go?'

The pair turned together almost bumping into each other but it was as if they had become magnets that repelled the other once they became too close. It was almost theatrical to watch. With Buffy in the lead, they made the short journey into the dining room. The brief from the incumbent Earl at the time that the designs for Manger Hall were drawn up must have been to make the building as light and airy as possible and, with the exception, perhaps, of the rather gloomy corridor that Bailey had seen on his way containing the portraits of the Manger dynasty, he had succeeded in that brief with real style. There were rooflights over the hallways and the grand staircase, light poured in through the conservatory, good sized windows gave light to every room, even the kitchen had enough natural light to double as an art studio, but the dining room was perhaps the crowning glory. The high ceiling picked out in ivory and giltwork depicting clouds and the tops of flowering trees and vines, laden with succulent fruit that originated from the floor level where they were painted on narrow panels in meticulous detail between three-quarter height panels of English oak. The southern wall was divided into three enormous arched openings, with French doors in each opening that led out to the patio and ornamental water garden which was fed via a set of sluices from the river so that the water level in the gardens remained constant. Even with a storm blowing up outside, this room was still light and airy and Bailey thought to himself; on the one hand, how lucky some people were to have a daily opportunity to eat their meals in such a room as this. It was a very different world to his two-bedroomed terraced police house in Exeter which he shared with his lovely wife Sarah and their three children. He thought he could probably fit his entire house and garden into this room and there would still be space to spare. He knew his Sarah would worry about him when he was late home this evening because she always did; it was her way. She would tell him off as soon as he came in the front door in mock annoyance, but then she would throw her arms around his shoulders and hug him tightly, and he thought how, on the other hand, for all the splendour of this room, of this house, there was much more of a feeling of happiness in the comparatively tiny space that he shared with his family than he had felt here all day; not counting for terrible weather, the loss of the doctor and the death of Lord Manger, of course.

*

Reverend Smeeton had done the constable's bidding and all the people that had been witness to the event of Lord Manger sitting on the nail, the event that, on the evidence that Bailey had at his disposal, had contributed directly to Lord Manger's death, were seated at the far end of the room from where he entered with Buffy and Gino. Buffy slinked into the room, unhurried and apparently without a care in the world. She addressed the other occupants with a non-descriptive smile and almost glided to take up the vacant position at the head of the table. Gino decided to remain standing some distance behind her at the shoulder of the huge fireplace that dominated the end wall. Bailey closed the door behind him and walked along the opposite side of the table, stopping in front of the assembled group. 'I know that you must all be feeling a bit shook up, what with the events that have happened in the last few hours and what I have to say to you now isn't going to make things any better, I suspect.' Bailey shot a look around the room and noted the reactions of the individuals; something his colleagues told him to look for when he was making a statement that would make the real criminals look uncomfortable. To Bailey, none of them looked particularly comfortable so he wasn't sure that it had helped him much. He pressed on. 'The reason why I have asked you all here is because you were all present at the time that Lord Manger had his accident this afternoon. You have all given me statements about what you recalled, which has been helpful, but then, as you are all aware, Doctor Macdonald arrived and examined the body and...' He paused hoping to indicate the seriousness of what he was about to say next. 'Well, he took a good look at the body and...' He was struggling how to put what the doctor had told him across to his waiting public. Buffy scoffed and opened her arms wide in a gesture of exasperation and went to speak, but Reverend Smeeton interjected.

'What is it, Bailey? What did the dear man discover?'

The clergyman's question provided both the focus and the impetus that Bailey was searching for. 'Well, sir, he discovered that Lord Manger died, because he had been poisoned!' The room erupted in cries and gasps. Buffy looked directly at him and thrust her head forward, her eyes bolting out of their sockets.

'What! What did you say, Bailey? Are you quite sure that is what Doctor Macdonald said?' Gino Vincenzi casually moved forward placing his hand on her shoulder as if it was the most natural thing in the world to do. She sensed his touch and was momentarily distracted, before refocussing on the policeman.

'Yes, madam, I am quite sure that is what he said. He wasn't sure how the poison has got into his body but he suspected that it was from the nail in the chair. We went down and inspected the chair which Mr Vaughton had put away in the storeroom outside which, incidentally, someone attempted to break into, by the way.' More gasps from the assembled company. Bailey was on a roll and continued to disgorge the shocking information that he had. 'Doctor Macdonald took a good look at the nail that Harry had left sticking out of the chair when he repaired it.' Harry Clott had been sitting quietly passing the brim of his cap through his hands as he listened to his betters talking. He looked up at hearing his name but Kate who was seated next to him put one hand on his and her other up to her lips to signify that he should remain quiet. He looked at her with a worried look on his face, but said nothing. Bailey continued. 'And we could see that the nail had something on it. It was like it was painted in something and the doctor took out his penknife and he scraped the nail and put the little flakes in his handkerchief and said that he would get them looked at by a laboratory who would be able to tell him what they were made of.'

'And where is the handkerchief a now, PC Bailey?' enquired Gino.

'Um, the doctor put it in his jacket pocket and then he left to go back to his office. But the bridge fell down, as I told you all, so the flakes are still in his pocket I expect. So we won't know what those flakes were but what we do know is that they were probably a deadly poison.'

'How can we be sure of that, Bailey?' retorted Buffy in defiance of the policeman's bold statement.

'Because it killed him Mrs Manger, so it must have been deadly.'

'No! What I meant was how can we be sure that whatever he scraped off the nail was poison? It could have been anything at all, including dried blood from my dear husband.' She held her head in her hand with her elbow propped on the table. Gino patted her shoulder and comforted her, but the scene looked wrong somehow as if either Buffy or Gino or, perhaps, both were just putting on a show for the rest of the room.

'The doctor was very sure that Lord Manger had been poisoned. He said that he had seen other dead people who looked very similar when he had been working out in Africa. He asked me to go and take witness statements of everyone that was there at the time and to see if anyone noticed anything odd about Lord Manger before he sat on the chair. He said to me that if the answer was that no one saw anything odd in his behaviour before he sat on the nail, then the only logical answer was that he had to have been poisoned when he sat down. I have done just what Doctor Macdonald suggested and I can confirm that not one of you noticed anything out of the ordinary with how Lord Manger was speaking or acting and then you all say that shortly after he sat on the nail he became unwell. So, even though I can't tell the doctor what I have just told you, I would tell him that if he was here, if you see.'

'I'm not sure you know a what on earth you are a talking about, Mr Bailey. Can I ask you how a long you have been a Police Constable?' said Mr Vincenzi who had moved away from Mrs Manger and had begun to pace up and down in front of the fireplace with his hands clasped behind his back like a lawyer in a courtroom drama.

'Almost sixteen years now, sir.'

Gino was pulled up short in his pacing by this reply. 'Almost sixteen long years and yet you remain still a police constable?'

'Yessir. I hope to beat my father's record. He was also a policeman before me. He was known locally as 'Old Bailey', he managed twenty-five years in the force without a promotion and my desk sergeant says there is every likelihood that I might beat him.'

'I see. And this is a good thing, you think?'

'Oh yes, sir, it will be a real achievement if I can do it.'

'From what I have seen, PC Bailey, I think it most likely that you will have a success in this record.'

'Thank you, sir.' Completely oblivious to the underlying sarcasm from the restaurateur, he continued, 'so as I was saying, no one noticed anything funny before he sat on the nail, so it has to be the nail that was poisoned and those flakes would have proved it. However, that is not important at the moment...'

'But what is important, PC Bailey, is that you are suggesting that someone deliberately put poison on that nail with the sole purpose of murdering my husband!' shrieked Buffy.

'Yes, madam, that is exactly what I am saying. Well actually not exactly...'

'So, there is a murderer 'ere somewhere?' said Kate looking about the room, 'an' you think the one that did it is in 'ere with us, right now, at this very moment!'

'What I was trying to say...' Bailey began to reply, but was cut short.

'Don't you think you should get help then?' enquired the maid anxiously, half- rising from her chair.

'Sit down Kate and be sensible,' snapped Cecil. 'Constable Bailey can't get any help because the bridge has gone, hasn't it? We are all trapped here together and we are going to have to make the best of it until help arrives from the village.'

Bailey tried again, raising his voice this time, 'will everyone please calm down and listen to me!' Every face in the room turned to face the man in authority who had just regained control of the situation around him. 'What I was trying to say was that someone did put poison on the nail, so they must have intended to cause harm to someone, but we must not rule out the possibility that perhaps they thought someone else would sit on that chair instead of Lord Manger.'

'I feel that is unlikely, constable,' the silken voice of Vaughton piped up from the end of the room.

'Oh, and why is that, Mr Vaughton sir?'

'Because the chair was set at the head of the top table, it would have been obvious to anyone that it was the chair Lord Manger would sit on.'

'But it didn't look any different to any of the other chairs, sir. Who set them out?'

'I did, sir,' replied the butler without any hesitation.

'I see. So, in fact you decided which chair his Lordship would sit on?'

'Yes, constable, that is perfectly true. I selected the best chair for his Lordship to use, as I have always done, on such occasions.' Vaughton remained poker-faced in his reply. 'However, it is not inconceivable, and indeed, it would have been entirely possible, for someone to have moved the chairs afterwards. You see, I left the ballroom, once I was happy with the room arrangement, including the selection and positioning of the chairs, and only returned later with Lord Manger at my side. He had called me to his study, to discuss a staffing matter.

Reverend Smeeton cleared his throat. 'Well, then I believe someone else did rearrange the chairs after Vaughton left the room. You see, PC Bailey, you asked me earlier if I could recall what happened around the time of the incident involving his Lordship and, at the time, I said that I couldn't remember exactly what I had seen. But I have had time to ponder and I am certain that, when I came into the ballroom I noticed the chairs were quite haphazardly spaced and, well, it's a thing of mine, but I like to see even spaces…, you wouldn't credit how long I spend getting the hymn numbers to line up on the board for my services…,' He cast a quick look around the room and realised this probably wasn't the time to have bothered to tell everyone about one of his foibles. He gave a small cough and continued. 'Anyway, as I said, the chairs were uneven so I moved them along just to get them to align with each other properly, so there is a possibility that I changed the order of the chairs from that which Vaughton originally intended.'

'That's very interesting, your reverendship. So, you think you might have made the final decision?'

'Actually, no, not quite, because Lady Manger wasn't happy with the look of the chairs, in the middle section of the table, and had Harry and Kate move the ones with the better looking red backs around with the ones which have more gold on them. Isn't that true, Buffy?'

'I can't remember now and I resent your tone, Cecil!'

'I was just trying to clarify things for the constable, Buffy. I wasn't making any suggestion of wrongdoing, but he is, after all, trying to build up a picture of what happened this afternoon and I think he needs all of the help he can get, quite frankly!'

'Thank you, sir, very kind.' Bailey smiled in the direction of the vicar. Gino shrugged his shoulders and shook his head in disbelief. 'That has helped clear up where people were, though I don't think you have told me yet where you were, Mr Vincenzi?'

'Of course, PC Bailey, allow a me to clarify. I came over to Manger Hall about noon. I saw Lord Manger and we spoke about some a very interesting business opportunities for a short while and then, he left me to go and do a something and I went into the ballroom. The tables and chairs were all set out when I got there, I didn't go near them.'

'Yes, you did. You were messin' about under the table, I saw you!' Harry pointed at Vincenzi, excitedly. 'It must 'ave bin you!'

''Arry's right, I saw you an' all. You was on all fours under the big tablecloth,' added Kate.

'Well, sir?' enquired Bailey to the restauranteur, who was already smiling at the allegations.

'As I say, PC Bailey, I did NOT touch thee chairs in the room. I simply lost a my pin from my jacket.'

'Your pin, sir?'

'Yes, constable, I have a small pin here, you see?' Gino grabbed his lapel and thrust it in the direction of Bailey. 'It is a small a red rose. I wear it to remember my mama and, also because it is the name of my restaurant. I think it looks very fine and I saw it fall out of, how do you say... the "corner of my eye"? Such a strange English phrase don't you a think, yes...? Anyhow, I tried to catch it but it fell on the floor somewhere in front of the table. I had to get down on the all fours to find it. That is why I was under the table, not to poison the chair, you understand, now?'

'Hmm, one last question for you, Mr Clott. Did you mend the chairs in the ballroom or outside of the ballroom?'

Harry looked nervous. Kate moved over to him and tugged on his sleeve nodding her head in the direction of the Police Constable, 'go on, 'Arry, tell 'im what you did. It'll be all right. I'll stand right 'ere while you tell 'im.'

'Well, sir. Mr Vaughton asked me to look at mendin' the chairs that were a bit wonky, so I got me 'ammer and nails and took some of the chairs to the yard and mended 'em there. But I 'ad to 'ave finished all of the tables so I was behind on the chairs. I know Mr Vaughton wouldn't be 'appy if I didn't get 'em finished so I knocked a few nails in the less wonky ones in 'ere to save time me carryin' 'em to the yard.'

Buffy Manger decided it was time to move the meeting along. 'Now Bailey, if you don't have any more questions or announcements for us at this time, I suggest that we get on with the meeting. The rest of the village are waiting for us, after all. I would also suggest that, at this stage, until you come up with a theory on whom the murderer might be, if indeed there is a murderer at all, that we merely confirm with the rest of the village that my dear husband has passed away and leave it at that. Does that make sense to everyone?' A consensus of nods around the room provided the affirmation that all were agreed on this plan, with the exception of Harry, who was bending over as if he was looking for something on the floor. 'Clott! What are you doing there?'

Harry looked up. Sorry ma'am, it's just that I've gone an' lost it.'

'Lost it? What have you lost?'

'Me string ma'am. Me string off me leg, I 'ave it for to stop the mouses, but it's gone.'

Buffy looked nonplussed, she clearly had no idea what the young gardener was talking about. Vaughton came to the rescue, 'He ties string around his trousers to stop the mice and other small creatures from climbing up inside them when he is working in the fields or the barn. There is one missing off his right trouser leg. Clott, it doesn't matter, you are not going to be working out in the barn tonight because we have the meeting. It can't be far away. I will get the staff to look for it when they clear and if it still cannot be found, I would suggest you cut yourself another length of baling twine in the morning. That's enough now, Clott!'

Harry stopped searching and stood up and shoved his hands into his pockets. 'Righto, sir. I'll do that, then, it's just I 'ad that bit o' string for a long while now...'

Buffy issued a steely command in his direction, 'We all need to be together on what we are going to say and what we will not say when we meet the others. Do you understand, young man?' Harry looked up but kept his hands where they were and shifted his weight from side to side. He nodded.

'Yes ma'am.'

'Good. Very good. Now let us go and meet the public, shall we?

'Not just yet, madam, if you don't mind, I have something else to tell you.'

'What is it now, Bailey, the villagers have waited a considerable time, what further information can you possibly be wanting to give to us that warrants a further delay for my guests?'

'I found something, madam, which I think you would sooner I discuss here than in front of everyone out there. But, as you say, your guests have waited a long time so perhaps we can just as easily go through these letters in the ballroom.' Bailey held up the letters he had discovered earlier.

'Letters? What letters? Where did you find those?'

'They were in a pile of papers on top of your husband's desk in his study, madam.'

'Have you been going through his private papers? This is outrageous! My husband is barely cold and you are snooping about in his study, in my house!' The inference that Manger Hall was now hers, and hers alone, was not lost on anyone in the room, except perhaps Harry, who continued to look puzzled.

'When the doctor informed me that he was convinced your husband had met his death by poisoning, I remembered that I had seen a lot of trophies and things in his study when I met him earlier. I hoped that I might find a bottle of poison there, which would have, at the very least, given me a lead on where the poison came from.'

'There ain't any poison there, Mr Bailey, I could have told you that and saved you the trouble,' stated Kate, matter-of-fact as you like.

'And a how would you know this so precisely, miss Katey?' asked Vincenzi in his legal voice once again.

'I do the cleanin' in there and I ain't never seen any poison.'

'Ah, I see.' Gino was really getting into the role now and he thrust back his head and, very theatrically smoothed down one side of his already very smoothed-down hair. 'And tell me, Bailey, is this true what Miss Katey says, did you find any such a poison?'

'No, sir, I didn't.'

'OK, that is a good thing, I guess, but that doesn't explain how you came by the letters, Bailey. You say they were in a pile of papers on the desk. Were you hoping to find a bottle of the poison perhaps hiding in the papers?' Gino smirked, pleased at his own joke.

Buffy let out a sigh of frustration, 'Thank you, Mr Vincenzi. My opinion hasn't changed that you shouldn't have been in the study without seeking my permission but, nevertheless, you were, and you say you discovered something important during your snooping so, out with it, PC Bailey, what did you find?'

Bailey took a moment to compose himself and then straightened out the two folded letters. Holding them at arm's length - his eyes seemed to work better the further the subject was away from them - he proceeded to read out the letter from the loan company. When he had finished, he looked up at Buffy Manger, who was wearing the expression of someone who had just had a large jug of iced water poured down the back of their neck unexpectedly. She was visibly gasping for breath and had placed her hand in the middle of her chest as if in an effort to push life-giving air back into her lungs. Once more, Gino came to her aid but, this time, he was joined by Kate who skilfully pulled out a chair in time for Buffy to sit on it before stepping back in deference to Mrs Manger's Mediterranean helper. Bailey was relieved to note that it clearly wasn't a chair that Harry had repaired. Buffy, bending slightly forward on the chair, appeared to be regaining the power of speech.

'Seven...seven...ty, seventy fi, seventy-five thousand pounds? Here, let me see that letter myself!' Bailey handed her the letter, which she snatched out of his hands, with no sign of an apology and, with trembling hands, greedily read the lines of type repeatedly. Her face reddened and screwed up before she slammed the back of her hands hard onto the table, almost tearing the paper in two, while looking up to the ceiling and uttering such oaths that might be more suited amongst a road mending gang.

'I say, Lady Manger, steady on, there is never a time when it is appropriate to take the Lord's name in vain!'

'Forgive me, Cecil, I apologise. I will make amends, I will send an extra maid over to St Julian's to do the flowers next week, but you must understand this news comes as quite a shock!'

'Evidently, my dear, the maid will be most welcome of course. Now, Bailey, please read that letter again, in particular, the section about receiving Rose's money.'

Bailey retrieved the now dishevelled letter and read out the passage again, '*However, in light of the fact that you have been such a good customer in the past, we are willing to give you the benefit of the doubt as you assure us that you will be receiving a substantial amount of money from the Stimper estate.*

With this in mind we are willing to hold off the repayment of your current loan of seventy...'

'Yes, thank you, Bailey, that's quite enough. I don't need a reminder!' Lady Manger held her head in her hands.

'Quite,' the vicar smiled nervously at the smouldering Buffy. 'Now that's interesting, don't you think? How could Lord Manger have been so sure that he was going to receive the money? The villagers have yet to hear our proposals and then vote on them, only then will we know who is going to benefit from Rose's bequest. He couldn't possibly guarantee anything...unless he knew something that we don't?'

'Perhaps, it was nothing more than hot air; the man was full of it. Perhaps, the loan company, they give him very few choices, perhaps he made the best of job he could, no?' Gino shrugged his shoulders and held up his hands, but had no takers for his theory. 'What is the second letter about, PC Bailey, is it more unwelcome news?'

'No, sir, it's quite different.'

'Thank goodness for the small mercies, eh, Bailey?' Vincenzi smiled back at the policemen.

'It's different, sir, but I can't say if it is unwelcome news or not.'

'Get on with it, man!' snapped Buffy.

'Very well, madam.' He launched into the second letter from Hattenschweller's High School. This time, Lady Manger was not the only one whose eyes widened like saucers. By the time he reached the end, Gino had taken a seat and sat open mouthed, while Reverend Smeeton shook his head in disbelief. Kate stood whispering to Harry who suddenly blurted, 'a kid, I never knew they 'ad a kid. What's its name then?'

Kate thumped Harry hard on the arm and put her hand over his mouth. 'I'm sorry, ma'am, I was just tryin' to explain what the policeman was sayin' to 'Arry. I din't mean nothin' by it.' Vaughton moved between the two of them leaning in and saying something that brought them both to attention. Buffy looked daggers at her maid before taking a breath and placing her palms on the table in front of her and rising slowly from her seat. She gazed into space about half way up the wall and said. 'Thank you, PC Bailey, for reading out that letter. I am sure when you read it for the first time, you must have thought that you were on to something. However, the fact of the matter is that I was aware of its content and subject matter.' She raised her hand before the questions could start. 'My husband was a very generous man and some years ago, before he and I became betrothed, he was involved in a great many charitable actions. This was one such cause that he contributed to. I can't remember now the exact details of how he knew of this school, but suffice it to say that he did. Perhaps through a function or dinner, who knows? He was approached and asked if he would like to become a benefactor and, fund a child, who had been left with the school by their mother, who sadly confessed they couldn't cope with the responsibility of bringing up the child. I understand, that this particular child showed great promise, early on, as a scholar.'

'Did you ever meet this child, my dear?' enquired the vicar.

'I certainly never met the child, Cecil, and as far as I know, neither did my husband. I don't even know the name or if it was a girl or a boy. Of course, they would have left the school some years ago now and, as far as I am aware, the school never approached us again to fund another child.' Cecil Smeeton nodded his thanks to the reply. 'I would like to think that you are happy with my explanation and that we need say nothing more about this outside of this room.' A rumble of agreement went around the room, even from Harry who appeared to be paying more attention.

With no further revelations coming from the policeman, and with a story in place for the villagers, the party decanted to the ballroom. Almost at once, the general babble amongst the waiting crowd died away and all eyes settled on the Lady of the Manor. From the look on her face, she understood her new-found position in the community and appeared very comfortable with it. The table for the delegates who would make their proposals had been set across the room, very much like a top table at a formal wedding breakfast, while the rest of the ballroom, with its three huge crystal chandeliers casting brilliant light on to the proceedings below, was set out with large round tables bedecked in crisp white linen with the ubiquitous red flowers in evidence as table centres. The villagers sat in their groups, the invisible lines drawn between the factions who had made it clear over the past few weeks who they favoured and, perhaps more importantly, who they didn't. There had been more than one incident where a conversation had started in all innocence but, as is often the case when money is to be had, people have an opinion and, when a great deal of money is on offer, even mild-mannered people who wouldn't usually make a squeak, for fear of frightening themselves, turn into protagonists; championing their cause for what to do with the widow's money. Buffy Manger stood up and, the room already quiet, became as silent as a tomb, as everyone strained to hear her every utterance. 'Ladies and gentlemen, it gives me immense pleasure to welcome you all here to Manger Hall for this meeting to carry out the wishes of dear Rose Stimper and to hear a number of proposals on what to do with the very generous bequest that she left for her beloved village of West Mucklington Parva.'

*

Harry Clott was standing in the corner of the room. He hadn't wanted to sit with the other villagers because he knew that they would start asking him about the chair and the nail and he didn't really know what had happened. He didn't have a proposal, he wasn't even sure what one was, but he was pretty sure that he didn't have one. Anyway, he couldn't sit at the big table, so he just stood and smiled at Kate who was sat at the big table, albeit that she was at the end, rather than facing everyone else; it almost looked as if she shouldn't be there at all. He slowly slid along the wall, hoping that he hadn't been spotted by anyone, but he could see Mrs Manger turning her head around to face him even as she was speaking. The look on her face told him that he ought to stop moving and so he did. When she was satisfied that he was listening to her, she turned back to address the room. 'You will no doubt, all be aware that the river has swept both of the bridges away and so it appears we shall have each other's company for perhaps longer than we might have expected but, never fear, there are already a number of villagers on the other side of the river who are aware of our plight, and I am assured that plans are underway to get you all home as soon as possible. Those amongst us who have small children or animals back on the mainland, as it were, need to let either of my two footmen standing at the front doors know about your requirements. I understand they have set up some sort of clever relay system and they will get a message to the other side to make sure that someone will take care of things until you can get home, so please seek them out as soon as I have finished this short speech. We will then proceed with a proposal from our dear vicar, Reverend Cecil Smeeton.' The crowd turned to each other and the small comments exchanged between them soon turned the silence in the room into a dull drone once more. Mrs Manger clapped her hands and brought the room back to order. 'Now, I am sure you are all wondering why this welcome is not being made by my husband, Lord Marmaduke Manger. The fact is that, I have to be strong while I inform you, that he passed away this afternoon.' The dull drone returns and crescendos to an excited buzz. 'I know this must be a great shock to all of you, as indeed it has been to me, but I am sure you will agree that he would have wanted this meeting to continue, as he had the utmost respect for dear Rose and he wouldn't have wanted anything, even his own death, to stand in the way of the money.' She raised her hand to her head as if she had a headache coming on. 'Er, I mean stand in the way of us, deciding democratically, what to do with the money. Of course, I have just said, that the first speech will be from Reverend Smeeton but, I was forgetting that my dear husband had also made a proposal, so it falls to me now to tell you all about that idea, my husband's idea, which I fully support, which is that we should spend the money wisely on Manger Hall, not only to provide more social space on the ground floor, but also to enlarge the living accommodation generally and, my bedroom and wardrobes in particular. You may, at first, think that the house is big enough, but let me inform you that it is not an easy task to accommodate all the clothes and shoes that are required by me to be the Lady of the Manor that you all want me to be. In addition, Lord Manger would have wanted to install a swimming pool in the orangery.' Bailey nodded approvingly to himself that he had managed to get the name of the room right where he had seen Buffy and Gino standing so close together discussing that note, whatever it might have been. 'That completes my proposal and...' noticing the Police Constable standing nearby, 'I should say that Police Constable Bailey, here, will conduct the rest of the evening to ensure that fair play is done when we vote later.' She signalled to Bailey to take centre stage which, from the look on his face, it was clear that the fact he was going to be running things was a complete surprise.

'Ah, yes, thank you, Mrs Manger, your Ladyship. Now, ladies and gentlemen, if the bridge had not fallen down then I would have been replaced by a colleague of mine, Constable Fogg. However, he can't get over the river now so I will carry on until he can; hopefully that won't be too long. We have heard the first speech and now, from my recollection, it will be the vicar Reverend Smeeton to speak next.' Bailey looked towards the vicar, hopeful that he was correct. The smile and nod that he received from the clergyman told him that he was, and he breathed a sigh of relief. He looked out at the expectant faces of the crowd, unsure what to say next. He was very used to talking to people on the street but he wasn't used to talking to big numbers of people that just looked at him waiting for something to happen. A thought came through his mind. 'Oh, and if I hear anything more, about Doctor Macdonald's whereabouts, I'll let you know.

'What about him?' asked a thickset man, wearing a loose fitting green jacket and waistcoat, with a bold striped shirt under which had the collar open exposing a great tuft of grey hair from the man's chest.

'He was on the bridge, sir, when it fell in. I thought everyone knew that.' Once again the sound of conversation picked up around the room; Bailey picked up snippets like, 'I told you so' and 'he told us all that when he asked for a search party, didn't you listen? Drunk again I expect!'

Bailey cleared his throat. 'One other thing before we go on, and that is, perhaps, it would be a good idea if we all showed our thanks for Mrs Manger's proposal.' When the rehearsals had been interrupted this afternoon, they hadn't got around to having a show of appreciation for the speakers and Mrs Manger, Gino Vincenzi and the Vicar all looked shocked at this new twist that the constable had thought up all on his own. The result was interesting as, although the voting was still hours away, the total apathy and general grumble emanating from the electorate left Mrs Manger in no doubt that her proposal had, in the words of the parable, 'fallen on stony ground'.

As Buffy Manger sat down on her chair, she looked around the room with her, very best painted smile, in a concerted effort to conceal the absolute contempt, that she felt for these unworthy people. The very idea, that they had the power to decide, whether or not, she got her well-manicured hands on the money, really stuck in her throat. She went back over the words of her speech in her mind and, reflected that, perhaps, she shouldn't have added-in the bit about the swimming pool - that was Marmy's idea - and that must have been what had upset everyone, she was sure of it. God, her husband was still giving her problems even from beyond the grave, would she never be rid of him!?

A flash of lightning lit up the ballroom as Reverend Cecil Smeeton took to his feet and, with his black leather-bound copy of the Old Testament securely clasped in his hands, he looked out on what he thought of as his congregation - though in truth he had never had a congregation at St Julian's as large as this in all the time he had been there, and that included weddings and funerals. The accompanying roll of thunder in the distance seemed fitting as he uttered the words, 'Dear friends, today should have been a day of celebration for the generous gift that dear Rose left to her beloved village of West Mucklington Parva, and yet the day is tinged, not only with the sad passing of Lord Manger, but also with the loss of our own Doctor Macdonald, a man who has looked after the sick and dying, in this village, for many years. His fate we do not know, the mighty waters are strong but, if it is God's will that he should be saved, then it will be so. We must put aside whatever unhappy thoughts we have from today and focus on why we are gathered here together. I was there at her bedside when Rose left her weak and frail mortal remains and made her way to the Lord and I know that she would want us to use this precious money for the good of the community and what better way could we use it other than on the repairs to the church roof and bell tower which long ago fell into disrepair. This is our chance dear brethren to bring St Julian's back into our thoughts and, with every peal of the bell, we will hear a reminder of Rose's gift and, perhaps, when you hear the bells again, more of you will be reminded to come to church and worship in his name.' The reverend cast around the room and saw that many appeared to have needed to look at their feet for some reason. He began to sit, when he remembered the last and most important part of his speech. 'Oh, yes, and once the roof is repaired we can commission a new stained-glass window in the Lady Chapel with a red rose depicted in the glass as a lasting memory of Rose Stimper. I do not want you to show by applause how you feel about what I have said but I want you to look into your hearts and see that this is the right thing to do. Now, I can stay no longer; I must use the study to complete my sermon. I will expect to see you all on Sunday. God bless you all.' He pushed his chair back and gathered up the remainder of his papers and, with an acknowledgement to Buffy and the Policeman, he made his way out of the door, closing it quietly behind him. Vaughton saw his opportunity and moved over to Bailey and whispered in his ear, 'the refreshments are available, sir. Perhaps this would be an opportune moment to take a short break?'

The prospect of having a break from running the evening was an opportunity that he wasn't going to pass up. 'Yes, Mr Vaughton, a wonderful idea. Um, ladies and gentlemen, as we have now heard two of the speeches, this might be an appropriate time to stop for some refreshments that the waiting staff will bring to the tables.' Turning quickly to the butler for confirmation of this statement, Vaughton gave an almost imperceptible nod and clapped his hands. Almost at once, staff swarmed silently in, laden down with cakes, sandwiches, tea and cider. Bailey made himself comfortable at the top table and tucked In, he always believed it was important and polite to take what was being offered to you, he also thought that it helped mingle in with the crowd if you did the same as they did. So, he made a point of two helpings of cake, and a glass of cider. After a while he felt well and truly mingled.

Chapter Nine

Reverend Smeeton made his way back to Marmaduke's study. On the way, he bumped into the line of servants that were taking the refreshments into the ballroom and asked one of the maids to bring him an assortment of cakes and, perhaps, just a small glass of cider into the study. The maid nodded and went on her way; he continued to his destination. Once again, he sat at the big desk that, until very recently, had been the pride and joy of Lord Marmaduke Manger, and reflected on how things had gone. He felt that his speech had been well received and he had noted a lot of approving nods from around the room while he was speaking, but then who in their right mind was ever going to think that spending money on St Julian's was a bad idea? He opened his black 'n' red notebook in which he wrote all his sermons and thought about the amendments that he was going to need to add in about the doctor. He felt that perhaps he was tempting fate to write about the demise of Doctor Macdonald, but the policeman was adamant that, when the bridge collapsed, he saw him disappear amongst the masonry into the river and didn't see him resurface. He decided that he would make some side notes and, hopefully by Sunday, he would know for certain what had happened. He took out his pencil and began scribbling in the margin. He heard the door open behind him and, without turning away from his work, he pointed with his free hand. 'You may leave the tray over there, I will ring if I need anything more.' There was no reply but the vicar was used to serving staff doing his bidding and so hardly noticed. Anyway, he was inwardly praising himself as he finished off with a flourish a particularly good paragraph extolling the time-honoured virtues of the good man who follows the sometimes difficult and testing path of righteousness and ultimate rewards in the life eternal against the foolish man who takes the easy path by the wayside, becoming prey to temptation and eventually eternal damnation.

Scientists will tell you that humans never did, nor ever will, possess such a thing as a 'sixth sense' but, without exception, everyone at some time or another will get that unexplainable sensation that they know something is about to happen or that they are in imminent danger, although their normal senses detect nothing at all. So, it was for Cecil Smeeton. He didn't hear anything or see anything but he just knew that something was going to happen. He stopped his writing and looked up; the curtains hadn't been drawn in this room, which was unusual. Perhaps, it was because it was Lord Manger's private study or, perhaps, it was because of all the events that had befallen this household today; whatever the reason, he saw the window and he saw the darkness beyond and, in that darkness, he saw the reflection looming behind him, standing motionless, hands high above their head. He saw all of this, but was powerless to react in time. His assailant moved like quicksilver and, in the same moment that he felt their weight against the back of his chair, he also felt the oddest sensation on his throat. His first thought was that it was a knife and that his throat had been cut, his skin burned so fiercely. He could feel movement behind his head and then he was alone again, the weight had gone from behind him, his pulse was beginning to throb in his ears and the sides of his head were a mixture of numbness and pins and needles at the same moment. He brought his hands up to his neck which felt as if it were on fire, but there was no blood, it wasn't a knife wound, he realised he was being strangled, but the ligature was so tight, so deeply embedded into his skin that he couldn't get his fingers behind it. He attempted to swallow but nothing happened. He tried again and choked, but found he couldn't draw any breath. He stood up from the desk and wheeled around stooped over like Quasimodo stumbling from side to side. He couldn't see anyone behind him but still, whatever was around his neck held firm. He scrabbled with feverish fingers, clawing at his neck; he could feel something, it was knotted or tied in some way, he tried desperately to pick at it but he was not a young man anymore and his fingers were not as nimble as they once were. He veered sideways with his arms behind his head. His elbow crashed through the front of a glass cabinet, showering him in glass as he hit the floor with his cheek, but there was no pain from the impact. There was no pain from his throat anymore and, as he rolled onto his back and uttered his last gasp, he looked up and saw his assassin standing very still, their face studying his, as if he were like one of the specimens in the jars of this room. He shot out a hand pleading for their help. He saw them move to the desk and pick up an object, something shining in the desk lamp, what was it? Reverend Cecil Smeeton's pale grey eyes that had looked on so many people as he had shared in their joys and their sadness became fixed in death. He was beyond hearing, he was now beyond anything in this world but, if he had been able to hear for just a few moments longer, he would have heard the crunch of feet walking unhurriedly over the broken glass and, perhaps, even the sound as the door opened so quietly and closed again, but he might have heard something else as well...humming. Yes, definitely humming.

*

Rather than go off and murder someone, Police Constable Bailey took the opportunity in the break in proceedings to revisit the small yard at the rear of the house and, in particular, the storeroom where Marmaduke's chair had been placed by Vaughton after the fatal incident. Bailey chose not to think of it as an accident any longer; as he was sure that no one puts poison on a nail by accident. He was also more certain in his investigation that Lord Manger was the one who was supposed to sit on it. He only took one wrong turning on his way back out to the porch and prepared a lantern before, hunching his shoulders to stop the water running down his neck, he made his way across to the store. He took out the key from his pocket, unlocked the door and went inside, leaving the door slightly ajar. He had wanted to come back and have another look around in this room in case there was another reason why someone had tried to force an entry. He kept the lantern at eye level and moved from wall shelf to workbench and amongst the boxes stacked on the floor, but he couldn't see anything that caught his eye. He then moved his search to the far corner of the shed and was halfway through pulling out some old rugs when he heard a noise directly behind him. He whirled around and came face to face with a dark figure holding a shovel above his head. 'Mr Vaughton!'

'PC Bailey, it's you! Gracious me, sir, forgive me. I happened to be in the vicinity of this part of the house when I saw a light across the yard. I couldn't think who could be in here and then I thought that, perhaps, it was whoever had tried to get in here earlier; perhaps they had come back to carry on with whatever business they had in here. I didn't have time to fetch you, so instead I came across the yard and picked up this shovel on the way. I wasn't at all sure exactly what I was going to do with it if I confronted an intruder, but it was the first thing that came to hand.'

'I see, sir. You gave me quite a shock.'

'Please accept my apologies, PC Bailey. I assume you have come back to see if you can find another reason, other than Lord Manger's chair, why someone would have wanted to come in here so badly.

'Exactly, sir, but my search has been fruitless. I was just having a look at what might be rolled up in these rugs because these have been put in here fairly recently.'

'How on earth have you been able to determine that, constable? And by the way how do you know that I am not the murderer and that I was not just about to bash in your brains with this shovel?'

'Oh, simple, really. Firstly, I know you are not the murderer because, although you set out the chairs to start with, you didn't come back into the ballroom again until you accompanied Lord Manger. If you were the killer, you would have noticed that the chairs had been rearranged and, surely, you wouldn't have risked the wrong chair being in place for Lord Manger, so you would have had to come back into the room to check, but you didn't. Second point, there are no cobwebs on these rugs, while just about everything else has been here long enough to have been visited by our eight-legged friends at some time or another.'

'You're quite right, you know. I must say, I wouldn't have noticed that myself, but then I am not a policeman and perhaps you are not as incompetent as most people think you are.'

'Thank you, sir.'

'Now, let's take a look.' Bailey hauled out the rugs and, putting the lantern down on a bench, he unrolled them. Inside was a single rolled up slip of paper that looked as if it had been torn from a magazine of some sort. Bailey unrolled it and held it up to the light. It showed an advertisement for 'Sutton's Seeds' with a drawing of a bunch of multicolour flowers in full bloom under the heading of 'Blooming Marvellous!' 'Nothing interesting here, this could be Harry's, I suppose, or one of the other gardeners.' Bailey looked past the piece of paper to see Vaughton's face uncharacteristically wide-eyed, staring at the back of the advert.

'I think you should look at the reverse, constable.'

'Bailey turned the paper over to see what had taken the Butler's attention. It wasn't another advert; it was a written article. Bailey read it and looked up at Vaughton once again. 'Well, well, who would have thought it? I think our gardener friend might have some explaining to do, don't you?'

Chapter Ten

'Aye, aye, what's up here, then?' asked Police Constable Wanstall, as he slowed the Wolseley police car.

His question was directed to his passenger, Police Constable Michael Fogg, who wiped away a circular patch of condensation from the inside surface of the windscreen with the back of his hand and peered out, as the feeble wipers struggled to sweep away the persistent rain, and saw picked out in the car's headlights, the small crowd of people up ahead of him as they approached the bridge in West Mucklington Parva. He glanced at his wristwatch and saw that it was almost half past five. He had expected to see Bailey waiting for him, as he was late, but then thought that he was most probably in the kitchen, with a cup of steaming tea, keeping out of the rain and who could blame him? 'I dunno' he replied, 'but whatever's going on, they want us to stop, that's a fact.'

PC Wanstall pulled up in front of a line of people, wrapped up tightly against the weather. PC Fogg opened his door and climbed out. He reached for his helmet and cape and pulled it tightly around him as he approached the nearest person. It was impossible to tell if they were a man or woman, but he was judging by their size that they were most likely a male, unless they bred them particularly big out here in the sticks. 'What seems to be the problem, then, sir?' PC Fogg had to raise his voice and lean in to the person to be heard above the weather.

'It's the bridge, constable, it's gone;' shouted back a burly voice. The figure turned and pointed to the road ahead of them and, as the crowd parted, Fogg got his first look at all that was left of the stone bridge and at the river surging by.

'Crikey, when did this all happen, then?'

'Not sure, but at least an hour ago.'

The policeman took stock of the situation and enquired, 'is this the only way on to the island?'

'It is now.' Came the reply. There was a footbridge around the far side of the island, but that's gone as well. The only way across is by boat and that's impossible with the river as it is sir.'

'Have you seen anything of my colleague PC Bailey? He is on duty at Manger Hall. There is a big meeting there this evening and that's where I was on my way.'

The figure turned to Fogg and shook their head. 'No sir, haven't seen a policeman at all. There were a few of the men from the Hall out a bit earlier. We tried shouting across to each other, but you couldn't make out what they were saying in this wind. Most of the village are over there at the meeting; the ones left on this side were working or just didn't want to go to the meeting. We tried to call them on the telephone from the pub but there is no answer; the line doesn't seem to be working. We thought it might be the pub had the problem so we tried to call from Doctor Macdonald's surgery but there is no one there. Someone said the Doctor was called to the Hall earlier because someone had been hurt.'

PC Fogg took the man by the shoulder and bellowed in his ear for directions to the pub. The man signalled with his arm and the policeman thanked him for his assistance and turned and made his way back to the waiting police car and got in. The wind threatened to rip the door out of his wet hands but he closed it with a satisfying 'clunk'.

'The bridge has gone up ahead and there's no other way on to the island. The locals have tried to call but no answer; probably the line has come down somewhere. No sign of Bailey.' PC Fogg jabbed his finger to the left and continued, 'We need to get over to the pub which is off in that direction and make a call to the station. The bloke tells me that the doctor was called over to the Hall earlier, because someone had been hurt. Let's hope it wasn't too serious.'

Chapter Eleven

Vaughton and Bailey, fresh from their discovery in the wood shed, were making their way back along the passageway towards the ballroom when, for the second time today, there came the sound of a young woman in distress. The two men quickened their pace in the direction that the sound was emanating from and arrived in the inner hallway to discover a small crowd of people standing around the young housemaid that Bailey recognised from earlier on when he had almost run into the Butler. She was sobbing into her apron and a thickset woman in a cinnamon coloured dress had put her arm around her and was pulling her into her rather ample bosom. Vaughton took charge of the situation and, given that it was a member of his staff, Bailey was happy to stand back and observe until it was clear exactly what had happened to this girl to cause so much distress.

'It was 'orrible sir. He's just lyin' there on the floor!'

'Who is, child? Who is lying on the floor, and where?' Vaughton maintained his impeccable delivery but Bailey could detect both frustration and, perhaps, something else in his voice, perhaps fear, even. The girl, with the able assistance of the cinnamon woman, calmed down sufficiently to speak and, in between sniffles and coughs, she was able to inform her superior what he needed to know.

'In there...in the study...it's...it's the Reverend!' The girl broke down in tears again and the big woman comforted her again with a look to the Butler that said he had the information he needed so leave the poor girl alone. Vaughton picked up on the signals and left the maid in the care of the woman and advanced on the study door. Bailey moved to join him and turned to the people standing around who were also moving forward that they should remain where they were for the time being. He turned and disappeared into the study with Vaughton leaving a number of disappointed busybodies facing the firmly closed study door.

Inside the room, the two men discovered the reason for the maid's distress. There was a tray of tea things and broken chinaware strewn on the floor just inside the door, the tea from the overturned pot making a dark wet patch on the rug. There, lying with his back propped slightly against the bottom of one of the taller specimen cabinets, was Reverend Cecil Smeeton. His glasses were askew across his face like a comedian might wear them for a cheap laugh, but there was nothing funny about the bulging eyes or the gaping mouth or, indeed, the sickly bluish hue of the clergyman's face. One hand was clasped against the side of his neck and one leg was drawn up as if he was trying to get some purchase on the floor. Vaughton crunched on the broken glass from the shattered cabinet door as he approached the body.

'Careful there, sir. You could be disturbing evidence. If you don't mind, I'll check the body.' Bailey walked around the Butler who was frozen mid-stride, not wanting to disturb anything else. He bent over the vicar and saw at once that he was right to halt Vaughton in his tracks, because he could make out the string that was around the victim's neck and, unless he was wrong, someone had strangled him with it. He gently pulled Cecil Smeeton's body by the shoulder and tried to roll the body away from the cabinet. Vaughton, very carefully, came to his assistance and, between them, they turned him face down in the broken glass which Bailey silently apologised for but hoped that the good Lord would see that it was necessary just at this precise moment. Bailey saw that the cord had been skilfully knotted behind his head so that it would have been impossible in the time for the Vicar to have released it and so, supposedly, choked to death. Bailey untied the knot and realised that he had seen this particular cord before. 'Well, Mr Vaughton, there is some good news and some not so good news.' The Butler met his gaze and awaited the next statement. 'The vicar has clearly been strangled which is, obviously, the not so good news. However, the good news is that I have found Harry's string!'

Vaughton looked at the Policeman and couldn't decide if he was joking. Bailey stood up and held up the long length of baling twine looking over at Vaughton for confirmation that he was correct in his assumption, but the Butler wasn't looking in his direction any longer. He was looking across the room. Bailey was standing with his legs apart on either side of the body and he shifted himself slightly to follow the other man's gaze. The big wooden desk which had held the small pile of papers that he had looked through and discovered the letters earlier had been seemingly brushed aside, as there was paper strewn about on the floor to the far side. Now, there was just a single sheet of paper in the centre of the gold inlaid green leather top.

But that apparently innocuous sheet wasn't going anywhere, as it had been pinned through its centre with a paper knife which glinted and gleamed in the overhead light. 'Bailey approached the desk and examined the letter without touching the knife.

It was written in a fair hand and read:

I do not know how a man such as you, can be so wicked when you know the truth.

I want you to tell everyone what you know.

You are a man of the cloth and should know better.

Tell everyone or be damned!

'If I had any doubt before that this was a murder, then I don't have any doubts now. This is not the sort of letter you write to someone who you like, is it! Come along, sir, we must get back to the ballroom. Do you have a key for this room?'

'Not on me, constable, but I will get it immediately.' They left the room together, pushing through the gaggle of people who had gathered outside of the study, curious as to what fate had befallen their vicar. Bailey remained at the door amidst a barrage of questions, while the butler disappeared in search of the key.

'Ladies and Gentleman, there has been an incident and I must ask you to be patient and to go back into the ballroom, where I will be able to tell you everything that I can. Now, please make your way back there. I will remain here until Mr Vaughton returns with the key and then I will join you in the ballroom, thank you.' A few people started off for the ballroom, but a hardened group of stragglers pressed the policeman for more information which was not forthcoming from him. Vaughton reappeared with the key and, with some ceremony, the study door was locked and the key handed to PC Bailey, who then herded his audience in the direction of the ballroom. Once everyone was back inside and seated, he took up his position at the top table and brought the room to order with a single long blow on his whistle.

'Ladies and gentleman, thank you. I know that you are anxious and that you must have already heard some things but I am here to tell you what has occurred. You will recall that Reverend Smeeton made his excuses to leave the room after his fine proposal, saying that he wanted to make some changes to his sermon. Well, ladies and gentlemen, I can't confirm whether he ever made those changes but I can confirm that he won't be making the sermon now, because he has been murdered!' The room exploded in sound. Women grabbed the arms of their menfolk and some put their hands to their faces in disbelief, some screamed, some fainted. Men stood up and waved their arms in annoyance at Bailey's bluntness. He turned to the members of the top table and saw Buffy's reaction was one of horror, but she was already being comforted by Gino Vincenzi who glowered at him.

Kate got up from the table and helped with the swooning women, while Harry poured glasses of water and ferried them to Kate. Bailey blew his whistle for a second time, stopping everyone in their tracks. The only sound was of the women still recovering from the 'vapours'. 'I realise this has been a shock and I'm sorry for the ladies who have taken it so badly, but I thought it better to give you the facts, because that is all that I have to go on now. Unfortunately, as you know, we don't have Doctor Macdonald here, as he was swept away when the bridge fell down...' More swoons from around the room.
'PC Bailey, have you no heart at all, no feelings!?' Gino was incredulous.

'Yes, sir, of course, but this is a serious business and I am here on my own doing the best I can! As I was saying, we do not have the doctor, but Mr Vaughton and myself looked at the body and we are fairly certain that the poor man was killed with a piece of cord tied around his neck. This piece of cord in fact.' Bailey held up the baling twine. Harry Clott recognised it immediately and came over to the policeman.

''Ere, that looks like my bit o' string that I lost. Where did you fin' that then?' Silence had all but returned to the room once more. Every eye and ear was trained on the two people who were talking at the top table.

'I found it, Harry, around the vicar's neck. I think it's what probably killed him.'

'Don't you say anythin' 'Arry. It's nothing you did, you were with me helping with the tea, so 'ee couldn't 'ave dun anythin' with Mr Smeeton.' Kate looked up at Bailey from across the other side of the table.

'All I'm saying is what we found, Kate. I will be asking people where they went during the tea break in a moment but, in the meantime I think we should all stay together in this room because, as long as we are all here, then we can all keep an eye on each other and I can keep an eye on the lot of you.' Bailey thought that this last comment might frighten people once they realised what he was saying, so he quickly added, 'that way I can make sure that we are all safe.' He thought about reading out the letter that they had found, but he decided that he wouldn't for the time being; things were difficult enough as they stood. He sidled along to where Buffy was sitting very closely to Gino, who was stroking her hand. She had tears in her eyes and appeared very upset, but Bailey knew that appearances can sometimes be deceiving. 'I am sorry, Mrs Manger, this must all have come as a shock, especially it is taking place in your house, and all. I wonder if it might be a good idea to go on with the meeting, as no one is going anywhere in the near future and it might take people's minds off what has gone on.'

'I hardly think that what we are going to do with Rose Stimper's money is really going to take anyone's mind off from the fact that two people have probably been murdered, but I take your point that we are British and we should soldier on. I will speak and we will continue with the evening.' Buffy took a moment to compose herself and then stood up. 'Hello everyone, can you hear me alright at the very back? Ssssh, sssss, thank you. Yes, I think it is important that we continue with our meeting. I am sure it is what Cecil would have wished for and I know that my husband would agree. This should have been an evening of celebration and we must keep that in the forefront of our thoughts and not dwell on the terrors that have occurred. PC Bailey, for his part, will keep us all safe and we are grateful that he is here at all. That was at the request of my husband and what a truly inspired thought that was. I have looked at the schedule and the next proposal is from Kate Rimehill, our maid here at the Hall. I am as surprised as you all must be that she has a proposal but, nevertheless, in the spirit of fairness, we should listen, I suppose. So, Kate, dear perhaps you would like to tell us what you would like to do with the money, hmm?'

Kate Rimehill stopped tending to the ladies as soon as she heard her name. She stood to Lady Manger's right-hand side, at the opposite end of the table from where the policeman who had said those things as if it was Harry that had killed poor Mr Smeeton. She brushed down her apron and then looked out into the faces of the people from the village, many of whom she knew by name and almost all of them by sight. She often went down into the village on errands for the cook or the housekeeper and, not so long ago, she was also running errands for Rose, but that was all behind her now. This was her chance to let the village know what she wanted to do with the money. In a way, she was sad that the vicar was not here to hear what she had to say but, then, he would probably have just laughed. 'What I want to do with the money is three things, really. First, I think if we could giv some of the money to burglars, then they wouldn't 'ave to break in anywhere, cos' they would 'ave money already. Makes sense, don't it, when yer think about it?' There was a murmur from some of the people at the back of the room.

'Speak up can yer? I thought I 'eard just then you say give money to the burglars, ha haa haaa!'

Kate didn't comment, but carried on in a bigger voice. 'The second thing is nightlights, that's what them bats needs so they can see when it gets dark.' Buffy gave a cough and looked down at the table. Kate looked to Gino, who sat with a bemused look on his face as he slowly shook his head from side to side. There were sniggers coming from the villagers here and there, too 'An then I think we should let the cows roam free as God intended 'em too, not shut 'em up in a field, cos that's cruel.' The man sitting directly in front of Kate was called Simon Forester, a dairy farmer. He couldn't contain it any longer and let out an almighty roar and slammed his hand down on the table in front of him so hard that the plates and cups jumped off the cloth.

'Let the cows roam free, are you mad, girl, or just plain simple!?' he roared. His laughter was joined by others around the room and Kate could see that people thought her ideas were silly. She could feel the tears welling up in her eyes and she ran from the room, she was so angry and upset that people thought she was foolish. Harry watched her go and went to go after her, but he was prevented from doing so by Vaughton who stepped in front of him and indicated to him to return to where he had been standing against the wall.

'Thank you, ladies and gentlemen. Kate is entitled to her opinion, though I would agree with many of you that her ideas are odd. However, you will have a chance to consider all the proposals thoroughly after we have heard from Mr Vincenzi in a moment, and then you will vote on who you think should receive the money. Remember my proposal on behalf of my husband was the first that you heard and was about the extensive works that are required to this wonderful house.' She hesitated. 'There was also the one from the vicar, just in case you forgot.' Buffy chose not to elaborate any further on Cecil's scheme. After all, the man was dead and it seemed in bad taste to go over it again.

*

PC Fogg successfully contacted the Heavitree Police Station in Exeter. The desk sergeant listened intently to the constable and told him to wait in the pub while he thought about what he wanted to do next. Fogg considered his situation and decided that, all in all, it wasn't turning out to be such a bad evening after all. He hadn't been really looking forward to overseeing a village meeting and now, as it turned out, he was going to have to sit here in the Pig & Whistle, out of the wind and the rain, and wait. Meanwhile, the desk sergeant contacted the fire brigade to see if there was anything they might be able to do to remedy the situation. As it happened, there was and, within nine minutes, they were on their way up to West Mucklington Parva. They had recently been involved in a big fire not five miles away from the village, where a huge barn and some outbuildings had burnt down. The steelwork has mostly been salvageable and, as far as the fire superintendent was aware, it had been dismantled and was still on site. His suggestion was that, by using some of the farmer's heavy lifting gear, that they had rescued from the blaze, they would be able to get some of the longer beams across the gap and make a temporary footbridge to get the people off the island. It would be some time before they could get road access again, but getting the people safely back to their homes was the priority. A car had already been sent ahead to the farm to let the farmer know what they needed and, with a following wind, and a lot of luck, the superintendent thought they may be able to get the first beams in place before midnight.

Bailey and everyone else on the island were oblivious to this rescue plan but the cavalry was coming!

Chapter Twelve

Gino Vincenzi had bided his time. He had listened through Buffy Manger's speech, but then he already knew what the content of that one was, and he was more than amused at how badly it had gone down with the assembled audience, though, of course, he would not be telling her Ladyship that, at least not for a little while longer. Reverend Smeeton's proposal was more or less exactly what he had expected from the vicar; maintenance of the church, a stained-glass window, all the usual things. He noted during his speech, that he received a lot of approving nods from the God-fearing village folk and Gino had the vicar marked down as serious competition for the dear widow's money. Of course, now that he was dead, and out of the way, so to speak, well, that changed things and, Kate Rimehill's ridiculous proposals were almost laughed out of the room. He had planned, with Buffy, for his proposal to be the final one. He always felt this to be a good move because, it would leave his ideas fresh in the villager's minds shortly before they would be asked to put their little cross on the voting slip. He was sure that many of the inhabitants of West Mucklington Parva would have forgotten most of what had been said in the earlier part of the meeting. So now he waited for the nod from Buffy, who would make a kind introduction, and then his little insurance policy from the dozen or so people who he had strategically planted around the room to give him a little ripple of applause as soon as he got to his feet. All it had taken, was the promise of a free meal at his restaurant, and they were his to do with as he commanded.

Buffy completed her little talk on how the voting would be conducted later, and had also taken an interruption from the postmistress Miss Harriet Chapman who had just wanted to let Mrs Manger know what a wonderful job she had made with the flowers for this meeting. Buffy had looked annoyed at the intrusion, but had quickly showed her warm and friendly side once again, when she had realised that it was praise for her and her creative talents. Buffy could have left it at that and got straight on with Gino's introduction, but she couldn't resist informing everyone in the room of the reason for the red flowers and how her husband had bought her the painting and how terrible it was that he had passed away this afternoon and how much he would have appreciated everyone coming and, of course, she just had to give one more little reminder of her proposal, just in case it had slipped their minds in the excitement. So, finally, she clasped her hands together and, turning to her left, she finally uttered the words that he had been waiting to hear, '...and so ladies and gentlemen, it gives me great pleasure to call on our very own restaurateur, Mr Gino Vincenzi, to make the final proposal of the meeting.' She extended her hand and Gino rose from his seat accompanied by the seeded applause, right on cue, which, just as he expected it would do, triggered the remainder of the room to join in. The look of surprise on Buffy's face was a sight to behold; priceless - no not priceless, but worth at least one hundred thousand guineas of anybody's money. He could feel the excitement rising in his chest as the applause swelled. In just one glorious evening's work, he would be a rich man, a prominent figure in the community, and rid of Buffy Manger and her whining for ever! He nodded in great appreciation, waved away the applause, settled the room and began his speech.

'Dear friends, my friends. It is with a heavy heart that I stand in front of you a tonight, because it means that we have all lost a good a person, a wonderful person, in Bella Rosa Stimper. But we must be strong and a make very good business with her gift to us all, no? It is her last wish that her money makes a strong impression on West Mucklington Parva and that is why the idea I have will be the one a you will pick. On this, I am strong on the confidence.' The door opened halfway down the ballroom and Kate reappeared behind Vaughton. She was carrying a cloth of some kind and was slowly polishing a handful of cutlery. Gino looked over and smiled, but Kate continued to look down at her work. He assumed she was still upset from the reaction of the room to her idiotic proposals and Vaughton must have told her to come back into the room. As appearances are everything within a household, he must have given her a menial task to keep her occupied. Harry noticed her come in from where he was standing, and waved at Kate, but she didn't acknowledge him; she just kept to her task. 'So, it is the detail of my plans that you hang on my words, I know, so I will give them to you now.' Gino banged the table in front of him with the flat of his hand to accentuate the point. 'There is land to the south of our village...'

'It's not your village, you wasn't born 'ere!' Harry spoke out in a loud voice. Vincenzi was momentarily distracted but, with a smile through gritted teeth, he continued, 'this land is owned by two farmers who I have spoken to at many, many lengths and I have their promise of a sale for the right price. This is a good start, because I plan for to buy up this land.' He drew up his hand into a fist as if he had plucked something from the air to profound effect.

Bailey was sat close to Gino and had a grandstand view of his performance. He was very good, he thought; he could feel the passion in his voice and, as he had observed before, Italians make effective use of their hands as they speak. He also looked out over the audience; he noted Harry getting restless, he noted Buffy sitting with a big smile on her face, looking up at Gino from her position in the centre of the table bedecked in red flowers, crisp white linen and shining silverware, he saw Mr Vaughton come back into the room with Kate, which bothered him a little because he hadn't noticed the Butler slip out. Could he have been wrong when he told him in the woodshed that he knew it couldn't have been him? After all, he had arrived in the woodshed after Bailey had got there, could he have had time to kill Reverend Smeeton and then cover his tracks by coming out to find him? A sinking feeling and rising panic arriving at the same time were never a good thing, he thought to himself, and he poured a glass of water from a crystal jug. He was pleased to find, that not only were there pieces of lemon floating in the water, but also a quantity of ice cubes as well. He was pleased because, he hoped that the gentle plink – plink of the ice coupled with the fact that everyone had their eyes trained on Vincenzi, would guarantee that no one would notice his trembling hand.

'...and to change this land into something new, something exciting, something that will put our village...'

'I've already told you, it's not YOUR village. You are a nink-wink foreigner!' Harry raised his voice a little stronger this time and stood upright facing the speaker.

Gino; his concentration broken, dropped his convivial mask, and turned his attention, firstly, to face the gardener, and then to Buffy, with a look of indignation that she was doing nothing to control this outburst, especially as it was from a member of her staff. She didn't return the Italians' look, for once, because she was already looking sternly in the direction of Clott, but she didn't need to say anything because Vaughton, who like all good butler's seemed to possess a sixth sense, had moved smartly across and was holding Harry by the forearm and talking to him under his breath. Harry was not listening, but continued to look past Vaughton and stare at Gino. He saw that Kate was watching him as well. A low murmur rumbled around the room, but now generally satisfied that things were back in control, Gino let out a slow measured breath to calm himself down.

This was not how he had expected this part of the evening to go. He had put in too much time and effort for anything to go wrong now. He had them eating out of his hand and he wasn't going to allow this fool of a boy ruin things for him. He would have to do something about him; there was no way he could stay when he was running things around here. 'So, my friends, what is this exciting new venture, I hear you say. It is the golf, that is what I will bring here! Golf, a game that is already big in many places of the world, golf that brings many people and very much money with them, golf will change this place forever and that is what I believe La Bella Rosa would be wanting; something that will make a mark for good and for the good of us all. Let us get behind this idea because we English...'
'English! You ain't English!' Harry broke away from Vaughton and advanced towards Gino. 'You are a nink-wink foreigner and you don't belong in this village, not now or ever!' Gino spun around to face his antagonist.
'I am just as much the English that you are, my boy. My Father he was an Englishman, just as yours was! I have

every right to say I am English and that this village is for me and for you, my friend!' Harry continued to advance.

'Arry leave 'im alone. Come and stand over 'ere by me!' Kate was moving between the tables, still clutching the cutlery to her chest.

'No, Kate, he shouldn't be sayin' things that ain't true! That ain't what Rose would 'ave wanted, you know it ain't, you knew 'er bettern than anyone 'cept the vicar, and he's gone now.' Harry was now level with the back of Buffy's chair, preventing her from drawing it backwards and standing, she had to turn awkwardly in her seat to talk to Harry, with little effect.

'Clott! Well, really! How dare you talk to a guest in my house in that way. You will leave this room immediately and you will leave this employment, as well. See to it, Vaughton!' Harry wasn't listening. He walked past the clucking woman, now his ex-employer, and continued to advance on Gino, who puffed out his immaculately dressed chest and met the gardener boy head on. They grabbed each other's arms and began twisting together, in almost a weird kind of dance. Bailey drew back his chair to stop the fracas but Kate arrived at the side of him and so he turned to her to stop her first, because he didn't want a woman getting involved.

'You're a foreigner and you only want to make money for yerself!' Harry continued to taunt the Italian. Kate pushed past Bailey and arrived behind Gino while, at the same time, Buffy managed to get up from the table and grabbed at the back of Harry's jacket. Suddenly the four of them were turning together this way and that. Bailey tried to break them apart and other men were jumping up from their seats and moving around the table to help. The tight group of four continued to writhe together like giant snakes locked in mortal combat. Their movements were punctuated by shouts, sometimes from an individual and sometimes from all of them at once. Bailey continued to try to prise them apart from the outside of the tight circle, but they rotated and he was thrown into the side of the top table causing crystal to rain down in a cacophony that to all who heard it, knew would have been exquisitely expensive.

A scream rang out and the writhing mass stopped turning and broke apart. There was the sound of silverware dropping to the floor and cutlery spread out beneath their feet as they stepped back from each other. There were no more protestations, they all just continued to move apart, their arms no longer linked together, their faces showing confusion at first, Kate grabbing at a chair to steady herself, Harry looking down at the floor and then, Buffy began a long piercing scream that would live with everyone in that room for a lifetime. Then only one person continued to move; the same person with a knife thrust deep into their chest. They staggered before collapsing to their knees as the rest of the room looked on, the full realisation spreading across their faces like a wave as the body toppled forwards, driving the blade through the ribcage and leaving the point showing clearly, bright and bloodied, through the back of the jacket; the immaculate jacket of Gino Vincenzi.

Chapter Thirteen

The aftermath of the spectacle was awful and Bailey had his work cut out to control the panic that was rising within the room. However, to their credit, several men stepped forward and offered their help. He wasn't exactly sure what he was going to do now, but he knew for certain that he had to get the three people who had been involved in the argument into another room. His first thought was the study but that was still occupied with the body of the vicar. Upstairs seemed impractical and, come to think of it, he still had a dead body up there as well. This was a very large house, but it is surprising how quickly space can get used up once you have a killer on the loose. He opted to move the trio back into the dining room and, with the help of the butler, who he was now happily assured was not the killer, they arranged for several men to remain inside the dining room and at each of the exits, while Buffy, Harry and Kate were seated as far away from each other as possible. He considered fastening them to the chairs but thought that was going a little far and he wasn't that good at knots, in any case. He also arranged for the body of Gino Vincenzi to be placed in the study with the vicar and had the ballroom tidied up, while the butler arranged for more light refreshments to be brought in for everyone. The mood in the room wasn't good but, with the extra men now being involved, most people accepted that this was now a village matter and, as such, they would cooperate in whatever way they could, even if that meant eating the Mangers out of house and home.

Bailey locked the study door behind him and went over to look more closely at the body of Vincenzi. He had placed him on the desk and was already regretting his decision because he could see the dark blood pooling under his back and seeping into the green leather, but it was too late to worry about that now and it wasn't going to be his problem to try and clean it. A thought flashed through his head that, depending on how this turned out, it might not be Mrs Manger's problem either, for that matter.

Bailey wasted no time in examining the inside pocket where he had seen Gino put away the piece of paper that was causing so much discussion with Mrs Manger when he had discovered them by the orangery. He distinctly recalled how the Italian had continually struck the paper with the back of his hand while looking straight into Buffy's eyes. It was important, he was sure of it. He opened his jacket which revealed a brown/red stain across most of the lower part of his dress shirt and slipped his hand into the inside pocket and pulled out the paper inside. He was thankful to note that the sheet had not been touched by the blood and, as he opened it, to his surprise, a second smaller sheet of paper fell to the floor. He picked it up and read what turned out to be a note:

My dearest Gino,

I find it hard to write this note but I sense that you are avoiding me. Can it be that I have been mistaken about our relationship and that you have just been using me?

I cannot believe that anyone who has been such a passionate lover could have been faking it? You should realize that I have invested far too much into our plans to let anything happen now.

We must talk. I am always yours my love.

The note was unsigned, unfortunately. How much easier things would be if only people who sent evil letters to each other would sign the things, he thought. He took a look at the second piece of paper:

I heard everything that was said the other night. I will expect your support at the General Meeting; otherwise you are going to find out just how nasty I can be.
I will have great delight in telling everyone about your past and do not make the mistake of thinking that I would not do it.
Gino

Well, this one was signed, though, in this case, by someone who was now dead but it was a start, at least. Bailey read both pieces of information again and noted the distinctly different handwriting. He knew, of course, that people disguised their handwriting but, as one of them was signed by Gino and the other one was addressed to him, it seemed likely to him that they were from different people. He folded the sheets and checked the remaining pockets, but found nothing more of interest. He left the room, locking it behind him and made his way back to the dining room where he summoned the butler to join him outside in the corridor. He showed him the two notes. 'What do you think of these, Mr Vaughton?' The butler read the notes again and shook his head.

'I don't know quite what to make of them, constable. Mr Vincenzi must have seen something of significant importance and it would appear that someone found out that he had seen it and murdered him, whereas the other letter is obviously from someone who thought they were very close to him. I have an idea that the person in that letter could be Mrs Manger...' Bailey looked up in surprise but Vaughton didn't see him. 'But I expect you have already come to that conclusion for yourself. I can't see anything else, I'm sorry.'

'Ah, yes, sir, exactly my thoughts,' replied Bailey, covering his failings to see what was clearly obvious to Vaughton. 'Now I think it would be useful if I were to question the three individuals on their own, because I don't think I am going to get anything out of them if I talk to them together.' Vaughton nodded. 'I remember that there is an orangery just down this corridor. I will use that to question them one by one and I wonder if you would be good enough to sit in with me. Of course, in normal circumstances, I would be carting the three of them off to the Police Station and, they would be questioned by a superior officer with me in attendance, but I can't do that very well now so I will have to make do.'

'Yes, of course, constable, I will join you. Now, who would you like to speak to first?'

'Mrs Manger, please. I will go and get things ready in the room. I am right that it's just down there, isn't it?' Bailey pointed down the corridor to his right.

'Yes, sir, quite correct. I will go back in and inform that she is required under your instruction, to accompany me to the orangery.' With the slightest bow, he disappeared back through the doorway.

The orangery was both fantastic and a disappointment to Bailey, in as much as it was a wonderful construction of glass roof and sides with opening windows which he guessed you opened when the temperature soared inside this glass box on a summer day. It was really a very pleasant greenhouse; the disappointment was that he couldn't see a single orange anywhere. There were a few comfortable seats in here and a small rectangular table, where he could imagine the Mangers taking tea with their friends. Tonight, it was going to be used for a very different purpose. Bailey was sat for less than a minute listening to the rain hammering on the glazed roof when Lady Manger arrived at the door with her butler by her side. 'PC Bailey, I assume you have asked me to come in first because you wish to inform me on your progress in this investigation?'

'No, madam, not exactly.'

'Then it must be because you wish to ask my advice on how you should proceed?'

'No, madam, that isn't it either.'

'PC Bailey, the third alternative is not one that I want to ask, but I find, in the circumstances, that I must. Are you questioning me because you believe that I might be the fiend that has carried out these crimes, including, may I add, the callous murder of my own husband!?' Lady Manger's voice had become high and haughty as if she dared this lowly policeman, who had never moved from the rank of constable in sixteen years of service in the force, to accuse her of such a thing.

'Madam, please take a seat here.' He waited for her to sit and then sat opposite her in what turned out to be a remarkably comfortable wicker chair. He placed the two letters on the table in front of her. 'I would like you to look at these, Mrs Manger, and then tell me what you know about them.' Lady Manger shifted forward in her seat and picked up the smaller note. Bailey watched her eyes dart across the text but she showed no emotion on her face. She finished and looked over at the policeman.

'Yes, PC Bailey, in answer to the question that you are burning to ask me, the note was written by me to Gino. Neither of us set out intentionally to grow so close - I certainly didn't set out to do anything deceitful behind my husband's back - but I am sure you don't have to be the great Sherlock Holmes to deduce that we have been having a relationship and I am sure that you can also see that things were not going well, lately.'

'Thank you for your honesty, madam, it makes my job a lot easier when people come straight out with the answers, though I have been working on a system which I call 'direct questioning' but I don't see any need for that now. Looking at the second part of the note, I wonder if you could tell me a little more about what plans you have invested all this time into. Were you, perhaps, thinking of starting up a business together?' Buffy Manger smiled and shook her head.

'Gracious me, no, Bailey! My plans were not about setting up a business, they were about setting up a new life together. Plans to win this vote and take the money and leave England behind us and live in Florence, in Italy, with my Italian lover. There, that shocks you, doesn't it? But, all the same, that's what I planned to do. Now that's set your mind racing because, of course, if I killed Marmaduke then he would be out of the way. But here's a problem for you. Why would I have killed Cecil? He wasn't standing in my way and why would I have murdered my own lover? That would make the whole plan pointless, wouldn't it?' Bailey shoved the second letter in her direction. She picked it up and this time she looked puzzled. 'I have never seen this before although I am certain that this is written by Gino. I have seen enough of his notes after all, but this isn't one that he wrote to me. Whoever this person is has a history, a bad history.'

'Well, haven't you just said that you and Mr Gino had an affair? That's a history, isn't it?'

'Yes, it is, I suppose, but you can't think that he would want to harm me, can you? And even if you did think that, do you believe that I would have been able to murder him in cold blood?'

'I don't know what I think at the moment, madam; please go back to the dining room while I talk to the others. Mr Vaughton, sir, can you bring miss Kate in next please.'

Kate Rimehill marched in ahead of the Butler. 'So, I suppose that she said it must be me or 'Arry, did she? Everyone knows that you will stick up for the toffs, but it ain't fair.'

'Sit down, Kate, and listen to what the policeman has to say to you. No one is saying that you have done anything wrong. Now sit!' Vaughton stood over the maid until she was seated in the chair previously occupied by Buffy Manger.

'Now, Miss Rimehill, perhaps you can look at this letter and tell me what you think about it.' Bailey passed her the note from Gino. Kate snatched it up and, with a sigh, looked over the writing. It took her a while but eventually she dropped it back onto the table.

'I've never seen it an' I don't know what it means. It's from Mr Vincenzi, I can make out that much, and he's not very 'appy by the looks of things.'

'No, Kate, he wasn't, and you didn't look very happy when Harry started to get upset with Mr Vincenzi and, anyway, what were you doing polishing those knives while a speech was going on?' Kate opened her mouth, but the reply came from the butler.

'I believe I can answer that, sir. I thought that, by giving Kate, something to do, it might keep her occupied and out of trouble.' He looked down at his feet at this point.

'Well, that makes sense, to me, anyway, even if it didn't quite work out the way you hoped, Mr Vaughton. I mean, you couldn't have known that someone was going to take one of those knives and stab Mr Vincenzi, now, could you? Why did you stab him, Kate?'

Kate shot up from her seat and slapped her thighs in frustration as she replied, 'I didn't stab anyone, Mr Bailey, why would I?'

'That's a very good point, young lady, why would you? I don't know, is the answer, but perhaps you were angry for Harry, he seems to be a very good friend of yours.' He tried a smile in an attempt to make amends for the harshness of his last approach.

'Oh, yes, me an 'Arry are good friends. We hit it off ever since I came 'ere. Everyone says he's simple, but 'e ain't at all. He just needs longer to 'ave a think, that's all. People needs to be patient. I wasn't cross at 'Arry or Mr Gino, I was just worried that he would get in trouble if 'e didn't stop shoutin' like that. That's why I went over and the next thing we was all movin' around and then I dropped the knives on the floor and Mr Gino 'ad one stuck in 'im. I don't know what 'appened and that's the truth.'

'Miss Kate, let me ask you another question about Harry. Why do you think that he put such long nails in the chair so that they ended up sticking out of the top?'

'Oh, that's easy, PC Bailey,' said Kate, with a smile on her face as if she was a little girl who knew the answer to a great secret.

'Really? Go on then, miss, why did he do it?' Bailey could feel a breakthrough in the case.

'It's because, even though he's not simple, sometimes he's daft as a brush!' Her smile broadened and was accompanied with an animated nod as if this answer solved everything.

'Thank you, miss, that clears up that point very nicely. Now….' Bailey was about to launch into his next question, when he caught Vaughton's expression of disbelief. 'Er, as I say, miss, that clears up why he did it, but it doesn't explain the reason why he put poison on the end of it, does it?' He looked over for a sign from his butler assistant whose pained expression wasn't helpful. 'Anyway, I would like to talk to you about the Vicar, Reverend Smeeton. There was a break in the meeting just after the reverend made his speech, do you remember?' She nodded. 'Good, now I left the room, but I wonder if you can tell me what you did.'

'I stayed and helped serve the refreshments with Mollie; she's younger than me so I show 'er what to do. Anyway, we put out the first lot of sandwiches and then I went off to the kitchen to bring some more. We carried on doin' the serving until we heard all that commotion in the corridor and then people was runnin' all over the place. It was Mr Smeeton. Florence took 'im some tea an' cake but she found 'im dead…it must 'ave bin' awful, like, findin' 'im like that.' Her voice trailed off as she imagined herself being the one to have discovered the body. Bailey imagined it as well and remembered the vicar's bulging eyes. She put her face in her hands. 'Poor Mr Smeeton, he was a nice man an' always good to Rosie.'

'Rosie, who is Rosie?' Asked the constable, thinking that someone new had arrived on the scene, which was the last thing he needed, this investigation was well over his head already.

'Rosie, that's what I called the old lady Miss Stimper.'

'Ah, yes,' he replied, with some relief. 'I think I have enough information from you for the moment, miss Kate. Please go with Mr Vaughton now, I will talk to you again later, no doubt.'

*

The last of the prime suspects shuffled into the orangery. He was still holding his cap in front of him like a small child might hold a comfort blanket. He looked a lot younger than his rough complexion and rough clothes suggested once you got up close to him and Bailey softened from the hard stance he was planning to take. 'Now then, Harry, lad, there have been some terrible goings on and they seem to have started with you repairing the chairs this morning and Lord Manger going and sitting down on that nail. Then, after that, you lost your string - you were lucky that I found it around the vicar's neck.' Bailey held up a hand while he continued to focus on Harry, because he could hear Vaughton breathing heavily in the background. He didn't need to see him to know what he was thinking. 'I want you to look at something for me.' Bailey produced another piece of paper, the one that he found in the woodshed. He straightened it out and slid it across the table. 'Is this yours? Do you recognise it?'

Harry looked at the paper and nodded. 'Yes, it's mine. Me dad showed it to me; 'e found it in the parlour and kept it for me.'

'Yes, your dad's the head gardener here, isn't he? What's his name Harry?'

'Yes,' the boy nodded.

'No, I said what's his name, Harry?'

'Yes, that's right.'

Bailey looked confused and tried once more, 'I know it's right, but I want to know what your father's name is, Harry.'

'I know and I keeps tellin' you that you're right!'

'The boy's father is also named Harry, constable,' Vaughton interjected.

'Oh, I see. Well, that must make things much easier for your Mother calling you at dinner time. She isn't called Harry, by any chance, is she?'

'Course not sir.'

'No, of course not. Anyway, my point is that it was your father that gave you this and you say he found it in the parlour, so you didn't take it out of the magazine that it must have been inside at one time?'

'No sir, and as I told you, 'e found it, 'e never tore it out neither, it was lyin' on the floor, 'e said.'

Bailey picked up the paper and turned it over. On the other side was a section of an article. The typeface was small and there were a number of small passages, mostly beginning with strange words which Bailey had identified were Latin, just like the names on the specimen jars in the study. The article was about snakes and, in particular, the poisons that each snake produces and how potent they were. Someone had drawn a black line in soft pencil, just like the type of pencil that Harry had lodged behind his ear, around a particular passage *Ophiophagus hannah,* or king cobra. 'Have you any idea what this is about, Harry?' Harry mumbled something and fed the edge of his cap through his hands. Bailey leaned forwards and repeated the question. This time he heard the reply.

'No, sir, I ain't seen that before, I didn't know what it said, so I never read it. Anyway, I lost that paper when I was clearing up the carpets. How did you come by it, then?'

'I found it in the woodshed, Harry rolled up inside a carpet. Tell me, Harry, did you try and break into the wood shed to steal it back before anyone could discover it?'

'No, sir, I didn't break in to find that piece of paper. As I jus' said, I thought I lost it and so I wouldn't know where to look for it, would I Mr Bailey?'

'But you did try and break in, then?'

'Yes, sir, I did. I'm sorry, Mr Vaughton, sir, I never meant to break anythin',' but I thought if I could mend them chairs by knockin' in them nails proper, then that would be a good thing.'

'Thank you, Harry.' Bailey signalled for his assistant to take the young man back to join the others. 'Mr Vaughton, perhaps you would be good enough to come back here once you have seen Harry safely back along the corridor?' Vaughton acknowledged his request and, placing a hand on Harry Clott's shoulder, returned him to the remaining suspects. In a few minutes, he returned and, to Bailey's great delight, he was laden down with a tray of refreshments.

'I thought you might need these for your deliberations, PC Bailey.'

'Most welcome, Mr Vaughton, sir. Now, please sit down and tell me what you think of our three suspects while I help myself to these.' The constable wasted no time in helping himself to tea and cake (two slices).

'Well, sir, I am not a trained and experienced police officer, such as yourself, but I do have a good deal of experience of dealing with people and picking up on the nuances of their behaviour and, in my opinion, I don't trust that girl one bit. She seems to me to be hiding something, though that doesn't necessarily mean that she is a murderer; it could be that she is helping someone else like Harry Clott, perhaps. Lady Manger, on the other hand, spoke very calmly and honestly about her relationship with Mr Vincenzi, there was even regret in her voice, I fancied. If I was a betting man, and of course I am not, my money would squarely be on the maid or Harry and the maid.'

Bailey paused between slices. 'Interesting, very interesting, and I must say that I am on the train of thought myself. But what about the fact that, perhaps, Mrs Manger killed off her husband to be with her Italian lover and then killed him because he spurned her charms.'

'Yes, constable, that is an interesting scenario and quite plausible, but why did she kill the vicar then? What possible motive would she have for that?' Bailey polished off the second slice, a quick sip of very welcome steaming tea and then retaliated.

'I had thought about that as well. You remember the note that said about him being a man of the cloth? Well, what if there was more about that child that Mrs Manger said and, if there was, what if the vicar knew the truth but did nothing about it?' Bailey gave his best knowing look with eyebrows raised as if he had really hit on something here.

Vaughton dusted his knees and stood up from the chair, placing his hands behind his back. He took on a grave expression and addressed the policeman who was happy making in-roads into his third slice. There was evidence of both jam and cream at the sides of his mouth; he offered him a napkin. 'The fact remains that while I may surmise, pontificate and postulate as much as I like, it is you, in your capacity as a *bonafide* member of His Majesty's Constabulary, who must make the deduction and, to that end, I will leave you to your deliberations. '

'Thank you, Vaughton, you are right, of course, and I apologise if you think that I was trying to involve you in the deliberations. I was merely asking an opinion from someone else who has seen the evidence and who has been here the whole time. I will continue to maintain a blank mind and will weigh up the evidence a little more and then I will come and join you in the dining room in a short while.'

Vaughton bowed and glided from the room. He had obviously misheard the constable; he surely must have said a 'clear' mind, not a 'blank' one…

Chapter Fourteen – Dénouement

Bailey sat, deep in thought, with only the persistent drumming of the rain as his companion. He poured himself another tea and looked over the pieces of paper that he had spread out on the table. He often heard from other officers back at the station how, if you put all of the pieces of information together, they gave you a thread, a theme, something that linked them all together and pointed the way for the investigator. He looked away at the darkness that now enveloped the beautiful gardens and wondered for a moment what PC Fogg had made of the bridge being out. He would have telephoned into the station by now if he could find a phone that was working. They certainly weren't working here but they could be in the village and, if they were, then everyone back in Heavitree would know that he was marooned on an island in a rather fancy house, but none of them would have any idea that he was sat in the orangery of that fancy house pouring over some notes that didn't make any sense and that three dead bodies and the murderer were in here with him. He sighed and looked back over his own notes of what he had observed, but he hadn't seen anything untoward at all. Marmaduke Manger sat on the nail in front of everyone, there was nothing suspicious going on beforehand and he had left the room just after Reverend Smeeton on his mission to get to the woodshed, so he didn't see anything then, just Kate getting more food from the kitchen, just as she said she did. Gino Vincenzi was the shock, because he was murdered right in front of him but he didn't see anything more than everyone else in the room; the argument that was raging between all of them was so intense that he was distracted and was trying to get them apart. He had no idea that someone was being stabbed, how could he have known?

He collected his notes together and made his way to the dining room, past the two villagers who stood to attention as he came up the corridor, which made him smile. These men were really getting into their parts and, looking at the size of some of the young lads, they would make useful coppers out on the beat. He made a mental note to talk to someone about it when this was all over. Inside, the three suspects were seated around the big dining table. Kate and Harry were separated by Buffy in between their line of vision and both were looking sullen while Buffy looked serene, but bored. Everyone turned as he entered; Buffy stood up. 'Ah, Bailey, at last, it seems we have been waiting for hours. Do you have any further news you can share with us?'

'Yes, madam, I do. But I have decided that, as the villagers were witness to some of the events that happened here today, I think it only right that they should be involved in what I have concluded.'

Lady Manger looked slightly shocked at the thought they were going to be part of some sort of side-show in her own house, but anything was better than sitting here any longer. 'Very well, then, constable, lead on.'

The rest of the villagers were intrigued when the policeman and his entourage of thickset men surrounding the trio of suspects, as they entered the ballroom. They took their seats on the top table once again and faced the audience. Bailey didn't need to bring the room to order as the villagers sat in silence in awe of what would happen next. Just before he spoke, a footman came in and passed him a note which he read, nodded and tucked away in the top pocket of his uniform. 'Villagers of West Mucklington Parva, I have reached a point in my investigation where I believe I can identify the person who has committed the crimes here today, and you have helped me in this, and that is why I have decided to share my reasons with you all and, to witness the arrest of the guilty party. Let us think for a moment of the reasons why someone would commit a murder. Money, jealousy, greed, love, revenge; they are all good reasons, and what I have had to work out is why there has been three murders and which of these suspects has the motive to carry them out. Let us go back over the facts as we know them, Lord Marmaduke Manger made his speech at the rehearsal this afternoon and then sat on a nail which had been deliberately poisoned with the aim to kill him which it did. Harry Clott, has already admitted that he had been repairing the chairs and, that it was him that put the nail in Lord Manger's chair. However, he denies that he put the poison on the nail. Next, Reverend Smeeton was found strangled in Lord Manger's study with a length of baling twine, the same baling twine that Harry Clott admitted he had lost off his trouser leg earlier. Then we had Mr Gino Vincenzi make his speech about golf courses and saw Harry got very cross with Mr Vincenzi when he said that he was an Englishman and you will all have witnessed, just as I did, the heated argument that took place, right here beside this table, during which Mr Gino received a fatal stab wound in his chest and died. Three deaths, ladies and gentlemen, but I believe that there is just one killer.' A buzz of expectation could be heard around the room following the constable's statement. 'During my interrogation of the suspects this evening, more information has come to light. Firstly, Lady Manger has openly admitted that she has been stirring Gino's cocoa for some time.'

'Really, constable, was there any need to tell everyone that information, and in such a vulgar manner!?' Even though she is a suspect in a murder investigation, this lady of the Manor was still asserting her authority, thought Bailey with some admiration.

'It is a fact, madam, and part of my investigation. Secondly, in the woodshed, I discovered a piece of paper which had been torn from a magazine or newspaper of some sort, which Harry Clott has freely admitted had been given to him by his father...Harry. On one side of the paper I saw an advertisement about seeds which, in itself is innocent enough, but printed on the other side of that paper was information about snake poison. Doctor Macdonald took away samples of whatever was on that nail, which, the doctor thought was most probably poison but, unfortunately, those samples were lost with him when he fell in the river after the bridge collapsed and, by the time we find him, they will probably be ruined, so it may be some time until we can confirm what was used but, all the same, it seems very suspicious to me. I also discovered that Mr Manger has debts almost as large as the widow's gift and that he was paying for the education and upkeep of a child that nobody seems to have ever met; very curious that he should get into such serious debt over a complete stranger, don't you think? So where does this leave us, ladies and gentlemen? On the one hand, I have thought about the fact that Mrs Manger was having an affair with Mr Vincenzi and, as I pointed out at the start, love is a good reason for some people to commit murder. But then, it is the death of the vicar that I find the most difficult to work out if it were Mrs Manger, so I discounted her as my suspect.' Buffy visibly relaxed and mouthed a silent 'thank you' to the policeman. Harry and Kate moved closer together and looked anxious.

'Now, with only two suspects to choose from things became a lot clearer for me and, time and time again, one name comes up throughout all of the things that have happened. Earlier on, I was puzzled by how I could possibly detain three suspects on my own with just a single pair of handcuffs but, luckily, some of you came forward and have lent a hand in helping me, and now I only have one person to put the cuffs on until we can get that person down to Heavitree Station for further questioning. Oh, and before I say who that person is, I received a note from one of the staff to say that there are men working on building a temporary bridge and that the first beam has already been successfully laid across the gap, so it shouldn't be too long before we can all get off this island and, you will all be able to go home...that is with the exception of one person, who will be coming with me, won't you, Harry?'

Harry Clott jumped up from his chair almost as quickly as Lord Manger had done earlier. 'It wasn't me! 'Ow can you think it was me? I never not liked that nink-wink foreigner, but I din't kill 'im, never!'

'Come along quietly, Harry, you can't escape from us all in this room, so just be sensible.' The men began to close in on Harry, who tried to bolt through the middle, but three of them held him fast. Bailey edged his way through the chairs and drew Harry's hands behind his back and snapped on the handcuffs.

'No, you've got this wrong, Mr Bailey, I never did anythin' I liked the reverend and 'e liked me!' Harry dropped to his knees and began to weep. The two burly men hauled him to his feet and half walked, half dragged him to the door. Bailey moved to bring up the rear of this sorry procession.

'Wait, I want to say something!' A voice rang out above the noise as the conversations began to mount. It was a clear voice, spoken with good diction, an educated voice, a female voice. Bailey turned, half expecting to see Buffy Manger perhaps rising from her seat to speak in defence of the boy. But Buffy wasn't looking in the direction of the constable at all. She was instead looking at the other end of the table where Kate Rimehill stood with her fingertips resting on the white linen tablecloth.

'Yes, miss Kate, what did you want to say?' asked Bailey.

Kate sighed, a deep sigh, and then she spoke, softly, clearly and without a hint of the common maid's vernacular that she had previously used. 'What I want to tell you is that you should let Harry go, because if you don't then you are going to waste a great deal of time and effort and, eventually, you are going to find out that he didn't do anything. The reason why I know this, PC Bailey, is because ....it was me.' The whole room breathed in and went silent.

'Do you know what you're say -'

'Don't interrupt me, Mr Policeman!' Kate leaned heavily on flattened palms and glared at Bailey. Her eyes glistened like coal. 'It's my turn to speak now and your turn to listen, all of you.' She cast an icy glance around the room, but she didn't need to worry about people listening; they were all transfixed, spellbound. 'I was the child in that school in Brighton, and all of my childhood memories are from there, that school. I have no family recollections, no happy times with my parents, because no one ever visited me or wrote to me or sent me presents on my birthday or Christmas, nothing. Of course, the school did their best but it wasn't the same and when other children went home I stayed behind and helped that crazy old woman, Miss Hattenschweller, with the jobs around the school. But I still had a lot of time in the holidays on my own - Miss Hattenschweller was far too old to take me out and she probably wouldn't have in any case, so I amused myself. I used to sit in the library for days on end looking at anything and everything. I was particularly interested in finding out about India, where I had been told that my father was working, doing "important work for the British Government". I read everything I could about the geography, the culture, the people, as well as the plants and the wildlife. I was especially interested in the wildlife and, one day, I was reading about its most dangerous creatures, like the tigers and the snakes. An idea just popped into my head that, if I couldn't see my father and where he lived, then perhaps I could have a little bit of India with me at the school. Miss Hattenschweller was eccentric but I was pretty sure that she would never allow me to have a tiger so I asked instead if I could have a snake and keep it in my room. The old girl put up a bit of resistance, but I can be persuasive when I need to be and, in the end, she let me. I used her account at Harrods and bought my very own king cobra and a big glass tank with a heater to keep it in. I waited for about a week and then, one Thursday afternoon in the middle of August, a very smart green van with gold writing turned up at the school gates with a delivery for "Kate"; just "Kate" because I didn't have a surname, I had never been given one, the reason for that will become clear in a while. As I got older, I asked questions about my mother and I was told that she had apparently passed away giving birth to me, I asked why I had never heard from my father and Miss Hattenschweller told me that he called occasionally but, unfortunately, never when I was around to be able to speak to him; very convenient. Time passed and my thoughts about my father changed from being fanciful images of him riding on the back of a great elephant to the image of a man who had built a new life for himself after the death of my mother, a new life in which I didn't feature at all. In the end I came to resent him, and then to loathe him, for turning his back on me and I hatched a plan that, after all these years, if I ever saw him I would kill him for the pain that he had caused me. I pondered on how I might do it and then, while I sat on my bed, I realised that the answer was there all the time. I had read up everything there was to know about snakes and it wasn't very difficult at all to extract a quantity of venom from my snake into a small bottle which I kept hidden with my most treasured possessions. I also thought about what my name might be. I checked the "who's who" in case my father was perhaps an eminent scientist or perhaps high up in the Governor's office or, perhaps, even the Governor himself, but I couldn't decide which man sounded like my father. I expected to be able to read about him and pick him out, but it didn't work. So, I started inventing names for myself. Grantham was nice and I used it for a while. Symes had a ring to it, but sounded like slime. Then there was Farquharson, but I couldn't get on with it and, eventually, I thought what if my father was a secret agent of some kind; he would have a secret name and so after some hard thinking I arrived at the name of Rimehill, which makes me smile every time I hear someone use it and more than ever after this evening.' She looked at Bailey, then to Buffy and, finally to the villagers, but there was no reaction. She shrugged and continued.

'Ah, well, it probably is too clever for anyone here, something else to revisit later. So, I had just had my fifteenth birthday, when I was called in to the Headmistress's office and she informed me that my time at the school had come to an end. In her words, I "needed to broaden my experience", and the very next day I was packed off to live here at Manger Hall. As I travelled down I thought about how wonderful it was going to be living in a fine house with servants looking after me. Imagine my surprise to find out that I was one of the servants! But do you know something? It didn't matter. I soon found out that I had a place in life, I found friends with the other staff and I didn't mind the work at all, I was used to doing a lot more at the school and Lord Manger was very kind to me. Within a short while of being here, I met Reverend Smeeton while I was on an errand in the village. He seemed very nice and when Harry, who I had become good friends with, said that he was going to church on Sunday, I said that I would like to join him and so I did and went to church on every Sunday that I was free. It was at the church that I saw Rose Stimper; she always sat alone and I was curious to meet her and one day I walked up and sat next to her. She smiled and at the end of the service I helped walk her back to her lovely home, Rose Cottage. I could see from her house that, although it was tidy, she needed a helping hand from time to time and so, whenever I could, I would drop in to see her, run any errands for her and tidy up the cottage. I bumped into Lord Manger coming out of her front door one morning and he looked cross and asked me what I was doing there. I was frightened that he was going to shout at me but instead when I told him that I often visited, he smiled and patted my head and said that I should come whenever I liked. I often saw Reverend Smeeton at her home as well.

Rose was already quite unsteady on her feet when I met her but, over the coming years, I could see she was getting worse, although, whenever I asked her if she felt alright, she would always just nod and say, "never better my dear, never better". But then she started to take to her bed more frequently until, one morning, I took her in a cup of tea and she softly took my hand and told me that I needed to get Mr Smeeton and that I shouldn't be too long with my errand. I didn't know what she meant, but I went as quickly as I could and found him in the graveyard and brought him back to her house with me. He went to her bedside and I could see from the way they were both looking at me that they had things to discuss, so I went and busied myself in the sitting room. I was just arranging the cushions on the sofa when I realised that I could hear the two of them talking through the gap around the door frame. I didn't mean to eavesdrop, but I wanted to make sure that Rose was all right and I was also a little bit curious about what they had to talk about without me in the room. And that's when I heard it.' Kate stopped as if she was struggling to keep her composure.

'Heard what, Katie?' said Harry, with his hands still cuffed behind his back.

'I heard the truth, Harry, that's what I heard. It hit me like a bolt out of the blue, but I heard the conversation between Rose and Reverend Smeeton as clear as a bell. She told him she was dying and that he had to tell me the truth about what he knew, what he had known for twenty years and that was that my mother hadn't died giving birth to me but she had had to give up the child so as not to disgrace herself and also so that the man she had fallen in love with, whose family would turn on him if they knew what he had done out of wedlock, would be able to take his rightful place as the Earl of Banstead, the seventh Earl to be precise.' Kate's eyes moved slowly to consider Buffy Manger's face, which showed only disbelief. 'Yes, Mrs Manger, your husband, Marmaduke, is, or should I say 'was' my father!'

'But, but, that's too far-fetched, you can't think that anyone is going to believe you. I have never heard anything so preposterous, you - you are just a maid!' said the Lady of the house, with high incredulity.

'You know it's true. How else can you explain the letter from Hattenschweller's high school and the huge debts that Marmaduke has incurred? Do you really believe that he would have got into such debt for something trivial? No, he did it because I am his daughter and because, if he hadn't kept up the payments, then he couldn't be sure that the school would remain discrete, could he? Miss Hattenschweller might have just told me the truth, so he kept on paying and then when the debts became too much he had me sent here to work for him.'

'So, you made your plans and poisoned the nail, just like that, you didn't even bother to talk to him?' asked Bailey, his mind swimming from the information overload.

'No, of course not, Bailey. I told you that I had made plans to kill my father, but that was when he was someone in a foreign country. As soon as I overheard Rose's dying words, I ran from the cottage and came straight back to Manger Hall. I went to my father's study...it seems odd to say that, but that is what he was. I went straight in, I didn't knock because I wasn't interested in his answer. Inside, I found him talking to Gino Vincenzi at his desk. Both men looked startled when I burst in and Marmaduke shouted at me to leave immediately, but I told him that his meeting with Gino would have to wait because I had something very important to tell him about Rose Stimper. His manner changed at once and he asked Mr Vincenzi to wait outside. I thought he had closed the door behind him but it sticks sometimes and it must have jammed. I told him everything I had heard and that I wanted him to tell everyone the truth that I was his daughter. He was purple with rage and he shouted at me that I must think he was mad or something, and that I had no proof, but I told him that I would get the vicar to tell the truth. He quietened down and sat back down at his desk, drumming his fingers on the arm of his chair, and then he smiled at me and said that he had come up with a plan. He told me he would go to see Rose and sort something out, but I told him that she was dying, even as we spoke, and there was no time. He thought for a moment and then said that he knew about her plan to leave a good part of her estate to the village, and he said that he would get proof from the school that I was Rose's child and, therefore, the money should come to me. He said that if he did this I would need to agree not to ever mention that he was my father and that I would have to agree to sign over a proportion of the money to him, because he had paid for my school fees. He said he would have his solicitor draw up the papers at once. I pointed out to him that he should have paid the fees because I was his child and that I wouldn't sign any paper, the money rightly belonged to me. He became angry again and said that if I didn't do as he suggested then he would have me committed by Doctor Macdonald, saying that I had a mental illness and was going around telling people that I was his daughter. He said that it would be my word against his and that the vicar wouldn't help me as I was just a maid and he was the Lord of the Manor. I left the room in tears and we never spoke about it again, though he tried on many occasions leading up to today's meeting.'

'And was my husband correct in his assumption that Reverend Smeeton wouldn't help you? Is that why you killed him?' Buffy's demeanour had changed towards Kate, her voice now much softer as if she was seeing her and perhaps her husband in a new light. But Kate was far from the hard-done-by girl that Buffy was starting to believe she was. Instead, she pushed back her chair and sat down stretching her legs casually in front of her with a look of defiance written over her face.

'Yes, your husband, my father, was correct. I spoke to Cecil on more than one occasion, but he wouldn't change his mind. He said that, even though he swore to Rose that he would tell me the truth, he couldn't go against my father and wouldn't support me. So, I saw him leave the room, saying that he needed to do some more work on his sermon. At that point I thought I'd missed my chance, but then I remembered that the bridge was gone so I knew he wasn't going far and then, when I was serving the refreshments, Mollie came into the kitchen saying that she had been asked by Cecil for some tea to be taken into the study. I told Mollie I needed help in the ballroom before she served him and, when she took the sandwiches through, I quickly loaded up a tray and set off for the study and that's when I bumped into you, Bailey. Oh, how close you were to the murderer at that point, constable!' Kate laughed out loud looking straight at the policeman, before continuing, 'I went in and he was writing something at the desk, his precious sermon I supposed. He didn't even look up and just ordered me to put the tray down. I had found Harry's string on the floor earlier and had kept it because I thought it might come in handy later and indeed it did! I walked up behind him and pulled the noose I had made over his head and around his neck, and then I tied a second knot at the back so that I could stand back and watch him choke to death. He crashed around for a bit struggling for breath, it was comical, really, his hands clawing wildly at his throat, but he couldn't get his fat little fingers behind the cord, you see. At one point, he collided with the cabinets and broke the glass, making such a loud crash that I thought I might be discovered, but no one came. You should have seen the colour of his face; it was as red as those flowers!' Kate pointed to the table centre. Buffy stared at the blooms with her hands clamped to her mouth. 'And then, we come to Gino Vincenzi; your Gino as it turns out, Buffy. He obviously heard what I had said to my father in the study and thought he would try and blackmail me into helping him get the money for his golf scheme, but how wrong he was. I mentioned earlier how much it made me smile every time someone said my name; well, you see, that's because when I was trying to think of a surname, I came across the notion that an anagram of something would be amusing and, as at that point in my life, I had decided that one day, I would kill my father - and I hope the irony that I have killed him is not lost on any of you - Rimehill fitted perfectly as "Kate Rimehill" is an anagram of 'I am the killer'. Now isn't that clever?' Kate let out another laugh. Bailey took out his notebook and made a note to check later.

'Well, Kate, you have been busy, haven't you? Thank you for your confession, it has certainly cleared up things for me, but what do you expect to do now? There is no way off the island, so you may as well be sensible and let me take these cuffs off Harry and then come quietly yourself, no fuss. Talking of Harry for a moment, miss, I can't believe how you let me and everyone else think it was this young lad by pointing all the evidence towards him. I thought he was your friend?' Kate stood up from her chair.

'Of course, he is my very dear friend and he always will be. I was happy to point the evidence towards him because I knew that, eventually, you would find out that you were wrong and you would have to let him go. My theory was by that time I would have been well away from here, but I wasn't expecting poor Harry to get as upset as he did when you tried to take him away. I couldn't bear to see him that upset and so I spoke out. I'm sorry, Harry, that they hurt you and that you were scared, but I knew you would be alright in the end. Please forgive me, Harry.'

'Course I forgive you, Katie, you're me friend, best friend 'int yer?' Harry smiled as the constable undid the handcuffs.'

Bailey was busy on the last cuff and his assistants were all around Harry, as until a few minutes ago, he had been the prime suspect, which left Kate standing alone at the far end of the table. The realisation of that fact suddenly dawned on the men and the maid simultaneously and, as they moved towards her, she darted for the door and disappeared. 'After her, men!' shouted Bailey. 'She won't get far, though, there's no way off the island!' There were shouts from the men, shouts from the crowd, and shouts from outside the door. When Bailey left the room, and ran down the passageway, he found a servant lying on the floor surrounded by broken plates, the result, he presumed, of the unfortunate person having collided with the fleeing murderess. People spread out in every direction in the house, but Kate couldn't be found anywhere. 'She's got to be hiding outside. I want all the doors locked so she can't get back in and then get as many torches and lamps as we can and we will go out and find her. She has to be out there somewhere, she wouldn't jump in the river, unless she wants to drown, of course,' said Bailey.

People grabbed anything they could that provided light and exited the house from every possible doorway. The doors were locked behind them and people were posted at each and every one. The outhouses were methodically checked, but yielded nothing, the ornamental gardens, again, nothing. The search teams formed lines back and front and fanned out across the rain-soaked grounds. Surely it was just a matter of time, there could be no escape for Kate Rimehill. After almost two hours of searching in the rain shouts went up from the garden at the back of the house.

'Over here! She's over here! PC Bailey, this way!'

'Bailey was only a short distance from the shouting and soon found Kate. She was hanging halfway across the single remaining rope of the old footbridge, edging her way along, her maids' uniform tucked into her waist, the apron discarded somewhere in her effort to escape. Bailey shone his torch on her face. 'Miss Rimehill, this is silly, you can't make it to the other side; you must come back, the river is too strong and if you fall in, you know you will surely drown. Now, come back miss, you can plead your reason why you did what you did, the judge will listen, I'm sure.'

With the strength in her arms slowly ebbing away, Kate knew that this was dangerous, but she didn't share Bailey's idiotic optimism over what the judge would say. She would hang and she knew it; this was her only chance. 'Bailey, you are a fool, you know what will happen if I come back. At least if I make it to the other side, I will be clean away before you can get off to chase me.' She continued to edge along the rope, she was now past the lowest point where her feet had hung just inches above the raging water. She was strong, deceptively strong; most men would not have made it as far along the rope as she already had. But as she continued to edge her way to safety and freedom, Bailey's torch picked out movement along the bank. There were people there, lots of them, and then he realised that it wasn't just people, it was a whole line of policemen! Kate heard the noises to her right and her heart sank as she saw the line of lawmen waiting to greet her when, and if, she made the last ten feet to dry land. She knew she was caught and there was no escape. She looked back into the bright light of the Police Constable's torch, her eyes wide and bright, 'This isn't the way I imagined it would end, Bailey, and I don't understand how a bumbling idiot such as you managed to arrange this welcoming committee for me. I am sorry to disappoint you all, but I'll take my chances, rather than surrender!' Bailey realised in an instant what she meant, and shouted out in an effort to stop her doing what would surely be suicide.

'Kate, Miss Rimehill, no!'

Suddenly all of the exertion of hauling herself along the rope drained from her face, her eyes remained fixed on him as she released her grip and plunged into the dark waters of the Exe. She was gone. Bailey looked to the far bank and saw the faces of the policeman who peered into the water shaking their heads and saw them moving quickly downriver trying to locate her in the swirling river. Most of the search team on the island did likewise, moving along the inner bank, while some ran across to where the bridge had stood and waited for her as she came past, but there was no sign; just the dark rushing water.

Chapter Fifteen

It was another hour before the temporary bridge was sturdy enough to let people across, and another four hours before everyone who needed to get off the island and back to their homes had done so. Several policemen had joined Bailey in Manger Hall and heard the gruesome tale of what had gone on this evening. Bailey was bemused at how so many police had turned up on the riverbank, but was delighted to discover it was because Doctor Macdonald had not drowned when the bridge collapsed, but instead, had managed to swim for the bank about a mile downstream and, because of the information that he already knew about the death of Lord Manger, he had alerted the police as soon as he was able to raise the alarm. He had then collapsed from the exhaustion and had been taken to St Mary's Hospital, from where it was reported that he was doing well and would return home to the village the day after tomorrow. Vaughton brought hot coffee and cake into the orangery which had been turned into a temporary incident room. He placed the tray on the table and sat down next to Bailey who looked worn out from his efforts this evening. 'I must say, sir, what an outstanding job you made of this investigation.'

Bailey looked over at the butler with a puzzled look on his face. 'Well, that's good of you to say so, sir, but I am not sure the officer in charge will see it that way when I finish my report. I mean, I've had three deaths, one of them happened right in front of me, I let the villain get away from me, even though we were in the same room and, to top it all, I was in the process of arresting the wrong person.' Bailey shook his head, 'that doesn't sound like a good job, now, does it?'

'Oh, but quite the contrary, sir, it was your blatant arrest of Harry Clott, even though you knew it wasn't really him, that forced the real killer to show themselves, it was brilliant!' Vaughton winked at the constable and stood up, picking up the empty tray. 'Pure genius, if you ask me, sir, and that is what I shall be telling your superiors.'

Bailey sat, open mouthed, as the butler glided away over to the officers who were now taking charge of the investigation. He sat there and thought about what Vaughton had said to him, and thought that perhaps that's what he had done, without even knowing it. Suddenly things didn't look so bad and Bailey settled down to a slice of cake. He would just finish this and then get started on that report.

PC Bailey will return
In

'Murder before the Mast'

The Story so far......

Autumn 1938.   The Chairman and Board of the Black Funnel Fleet, are celebrating their 90th birthday and the acquisition of their latest and most famous addition to the fleet, Brunel's masterpiece, the biggest ship in the world in its time, The s.s. Great Britain. To honour this milestone in the company's history, they have thrown an extravagant party on board while the ship makes a rare return to the dry dock where her construction began in July of 1839. The event will be attended by the most influential people in the great City of Bristol.

The Captain of the ship John Nelson is already down in the bar and it looks like he may well become a handful as the evening goes on.

The Family Fortescue-Smythe are very well represented with the Chairman's Niece joining the party with her Fiancé Maurice Leyton. The Chairman's second wife Sara completes the party.

Everyone is expecting a wonderful time, but none are aware that during this very auspicious evening, certain people will have the shock of their very life. Who will this be and, why have they chosen to wreak such death and despair will unfold before the night is out.

Printed in Great Britain
by Amazon

37752901R00089